The Secret Summer of Daniel Lyons

is set in 1909 in a sm
Thirteen year old To
Methodist parents and
'Daniel Lyons', visits the
run by the happy-go-luck
a regular visitor, helping t...... ..... their film-making
and forming an unlikely friendship with
fourteen year old Laura Merry.

But how long can he keep up his double life?
And who are the mysterious 'busters'
the Merrys are so terrified of?
And most particularly just who is
the Reverend Ezekiel Snook?

OTHER BOOKS BY
ROY APPS

How to Handle Your Teacher
Scholastic

Stacey Stone
Scholastic

Ann Frank: The Last Days of Freedom
Hodder Wayland

Leif Ericson: Outlaw's Son
Hodder Wayland

Roy Apps

—

𝕿𝖍𝖊 𝕾𝖊𝖈𝖗𝖊𝖙 𝕾𝖚𝖒𝖒𝖊𝖗 𝖔𝖋 Daniel Lyons

—

BARN OWL BOOKS

FOR JOEL

First published by Andersen Press 1991
This edition first published 2002 by Barn Owl Books
15 New Cavendish Street, London W1M 7RL

Text copyright © 1991, 2002 Roy Apps
Roy Apps has asserted his right under the
Copyright, Designs and Patents Act 1988
to be identified as the author of this work

ISBN 1 903015 16 2

A CIP catalogue record for this book
is available from the British Library

Designed and typeset by Douglas Martin Associates
Printed and bound in Great Britain by
Creative print and Design Wales, Ebbw Vale

Chapter One

The small brick chapel was full to bursting. The air simmered with a sweetish, stifling heat that was beginning to smell increasingly of sweat.

Tom Jupe was dressed in his hated, itchy black Sunday suit and the sermon was into its thirty-fifth minute, but he didn't care one bit. With the forefinger and thumb of each hand he made a square, which he put up to his right eye while closing the left. Then he roved the chapel with his eye until he caught the Reverend Gilbert Comfort between his forefingers and his thumbs. Suddenly, with a tingle of excitement, Tom realised that he had framed the perfect photograph. Encircling Mr Comfort's balding, sunlit head was the huge frieze bearing the text 𝕲𝔬𝔡 𝔟𝔢 𝔐𝔢𝔯𝔠𝔦𝔣𝔲𝔩 𝔱𝔬 𝔐𝔢 𝔞 𝔖𝔦𝔫𝔫𝔢𝔯: *Luke 18:13*, and in front was the great dark oak pulpit. Tom stared at the minister through his finger frame. If only he had a camera! 'Stand steady as you are for two minutes, sir!' That was what Wilf Puttock, the village's professional photographer would say. And he would begin to count and hope the minister didn't move.

And then curse him if he did.

It was odd, Tom thought, how at that distance, Mr Comfort was small enough to fit between his finger and thumb.

A sudden sting of pain to his knuckles brought Tom's finger-frame down into his lap again. A large black-gloved hand crept back to its familiar place on the cover of a battered hymnbook. Tom winced. As usual, his mother's wedding-ring had caught him on the boniest part of the knuckle.

Tom briefly met her all-seeing glare. He knew that if he tried to hold his mother's eye, the photographer he imagined himself to be would somehow shrink away and he would become nothing more than her wearisome, wilful, thirteen-year-old son once more.

He quickly looked away towards the pulpit. The figure of the elderly minister had gone. The text and pulpit now framed an empty space. The moment for the perfect photograph had passed.

Mr Comfort was standing in front of the pulpit and announcing the number of the final hymn. The organ wheezed and warbled and the body of the chapel congregation rose as one. The singing was loud, though rough and ragged and Tom (because he knew a good sing helped to get things off his chest) joined in lustily.

Outside, the hymn-singing could be heard quite clearly. There was, after all, virtually no other sound – with the exception of bird song – to compete with it. It was just past eight o'clock on a Sunday evening in June 1909 and the entire population of Aduring-by-Sea, Sussex, was either in the Parish Church of St. Cosmo's in the village centre; or in one of the numerous side-street chapels; or in one of the even more numerous ale-houses that littered the harbour quay.

Except, of course, for John Jarrett Esquire, the stationmaster, who stood on the down platform, gold hunter watch in hand, listening to the singing drifting across from the Primitive Methodist chapel, just a couple of hundred metres away.

'Must ha' been some long sermonisin' at the Prim tonight,' he said, for the stationmaster, like everyone else in Aduring-by-Sea, did not believe in giving the chapel or its congregation their full title, when a particularly appropriate abbreviation like 'Prim' would do.

Four minutes past eight said John Jarrett's watch, as the sound of the singing was gradually, then completely, drowned by the hissing, clanking, screeching and clattering of the 6.10 from London sliding to a halt alongside the platform.

'Aduring-by-Sea. Aduring-by-Sea. Adur-*ing*-by-Sea,' bellowed John Jarrett. Each 'Aduring' was uttered differently; there was a gentle 'Aduring,' a gruff 'Aduring', an 'Adur*ing*' and an '*Adu*ring'. Some eight trains an hour stopped at the station, and for each train John Jarrett announced the name of the bustling fishing village at least half a dozen times. This meant that during the course of a normal working day, the long-suffering stationmaster uttered the words 'Aduring-by-Sea' no fewer than four hundred and eighty times. Which was why he tried to make each 'Aduring' different; otherwise he would have been struck dumb with boredom.

Five passengers got down from the London train: a large, blustering man in a Norfolk jacket and with him a tall, elegant woman and an attractive girl in her early teens. Just behind them were two noisy fellows in their twenties. While the large man was helped with numerous items of luggage by one of the younger men, the two ladies stood by and the other younger man bounded along the platform, straight towards the station gates.

'I say Joe, do lend a hand!' protested his colleague, but Joe either didn't hear or didn't care, for he was out of the station and into the village main street in no time.

There he stood quite still and sniffed the sharp tang of salty air that told him he was beside the sea. He looked up the road out of the village and noted a number of ugly new villas. He looked down the road towards the village itself. The winding street was crowded with narrow cottages and shops, all of a different shape and height; some brick, some flint, some rendered with grey cement.

Then slowly, deliberately, with the forefinger and thumb of each hand, this young man made a square, which he put up to his right eye while closing the left. He looked through his finger-frame at various clusters of buildings, including the tiny chapel where the last strains of hymn-singing had just died away.

The rest of the party ambled out from the station. Joe spun round to face them and caught them all as a group between his forefingers and his thumbs.

'G-G-Guv'nor!' he stuttered, in a voice filled with excitement. 'It's blinkin' hunky dory! The air, the l-l-light, the colours, everythin'!'

'Ah Aduring! Thou queenly port by Sussex's seaside! Thy name shall surely soon be known worldwide!' boomed the large man in rich, velvety tones, by way of reply.

The rest of the party all groaned, loudly.

'I spent half the wretched journey from London composing those lines,' protested the large man in mock anguish.

From the stationmaster's office window, John Jarrett watched the strange and colourful party pass out of sight down the main street towards the river estuary and the sea.

'Beach folk, else I'm a Dutchman,' he said in severely disapproving tones, shaking his head at his gold hunter watch.

Chapter Two

The service was over, the last hymn sung, and the late evening light was already beginning to mellow over the roofs and chimney pots of Aduring-by-Sea. The Jupes walked home up the twitten, the alleyway that ran behind the terrace of tiny cottages where they lived. Rampaging nettles, brambles and cow-parsley, heavy with recent rain, sagged and drooped menacingly across the narrow track, which itself glistened with chalky puddles, so that the Jupes were forced to proceed carefully in single file, like explorers forging a pathway through untamed jungle. In front walked Mr Jupe, dark-skinned, small and smart; and behind him Tom, dark too, and almost as tall as his father. Behind Tom came his mother, tall, erect and much fairer than his father. His sister Maisie brought up the rear.

At eighteen, Maisie was more than four years older than Tom. She worked as a seamstress at a draper's store in Hove, about six miles along the coast, and as such was for Tom, just another adult. Of course, when he was little, she had taught him to skip and to play hopscotch. Then came the day when Tom had suddenly realised that such things were cissy and girlish and they had hardly really spoken to each other since.

Lately, though, Tom had half-wished that he knew how to speak to his sister. For at supper, just over a week ago, Tom's father had suddenly said to him: 'You ain't 'ad a shearin' this week, have you, boy?'

'No, Dad.' Somehow Tom guessed that what his father was on about had very little to do with haircuts.

There was a pause while Tom's father hacked himself off a lump of cheese from the quarter round. 'Wonder who 'twas then I saw a-comin' out o' Jessup's 'sarter-noon?' Jessup's being the one and only barber's shop in Aduring. 'Looked jest like you, boy.'

'Was me, Dad.'

'Yes, and you 'adn't bin to see Jessup, you bin to see that young Wilf Puttock out the back.'

'Yes, Dad. He wanted to show me his new camera! It's a Fulmer-Schwig!' Tom's excitement and enthusiasm had been painfully transparent.

'You'd no business bothering him.'

'It weren't no bother. He said. Said it were a proper change to find a young chap serious about photographics. Said he might be takin' on a 'prentice.'

'He might be takin' on a dozen 'prentices for all I know, but not one of 'em is goin' to be you, boy!'

'But, Dad –'

'It's a new-fangled business with who knows what future – if any. Not a proper 'stablished trade, neither. You'll be of no use in this world without a *proper* trade, boy.'

'What do you mean, a *proper* trade?'

Tom's father ignored the question. 'Anyway, I don't like the man. 'E's gaudy and 'e's too fond o'talk.' Tom's father paused. 'Besides, 'e got no faith.' By which Tom's father meant that not only did Wilf Puttock never attend chapel, but he never visited the church either.

Tom had briefly caught his mother's eye, but she had only nodded slightly, as if in total agreement with her husband. In the Jupe household, there were two sets of utterances that were never in dispute: the Word of God as delivered to Man between the black covers of the Holy

Bible and the word of Mr Jupe as delivered to Mrs Jupe, Maisie and Tom between pickled onions at supper. It was not that Mr Jupe was a tyrant or an ogre, it was just that this was the way of things for a 'Prim' family.

'When the time comes, you'll go to work 'longside me at Larcombe's as a 'prentice.' Tom's father was a carpenter with a small local firm. Sometimes he built doors and window frames for people about to move into one of Aduring's new brick villas. More often, though, he found himself building coffins for people about to move into St. Cosmo's churchyard. 'Carpentry's not one of these johnny-come-lately affairs. A good joiner'll always be in work.'

To mark the fact that the subject was now closed, Tom's father had picked up his fork, thrust it into the bottle that sat by his plate and speared another pickled onion.

'When the time comes . . .' Phrases such as 'when the time comes you'll go to work 'longside me' had been familiar to Tom ever since he could remember, but now a feeling of sheer panic welled up inside him, for, all of a sudden it seemed, 'the time' had 'come'. It had crept up behind him and had tapped him on the shoulder. It was now the middle of the summer term. Tom was to leave school and start work the following Easter, a few weeks after his fourteenth birthday. Easter. It had seemed to him to be just a few – too few – tomorrows away.

A desperate leaden feeling had gripped the pit of Tom's stomach as he saw his future – his entire life – laid out before him. Working in the joinery shop, just like his father had done; marrying a nice quiet chapel girl, just like his father had done; teaching in Sunday School, just like his father had done; living a life bounded by chapel and work, just like father had done. There and then, Tom had realised with a frightening certainty that he wanted something else, something *different*.

Now, a week later, that feeling of panic had gone, to be

replaced by one of dull acceptance. This was his world, after all, bounded to the north by the green pastures of the Downs, to the west by the wide, winding river; to the south by the sea and to the east by the twin resorts of Brighton and Hove. His world was nothing more, nothing less than a picture frame, and he was the subject frozen for all time within it.

In truth though, Aduring-by-Sea was not one world, but three worlds. At the back, the old village of Aduring, nestling under the Downs, contained rural, farming folk, who still thought of themselves as living in Aduring *Proper*. This was where both of Tom's grandfathers and his grand-mother lived.

The 'new' larger village, where Tom himself lived, had grown up when the river had silted up, making it unnavigable to all but the most shallow drafted dinghies. Over the years it had spread itself all the way along the river estuary to the harbour quay. The people here, in the main, drew their living directly or indirectly from the river and the sea – fishermen, boat builders, chandlers, rope-makers.

Across the river estuary from the two Aduring villages was Aduring Beach, a peninsula of land about a mile and a half long and a quarter of a mile wide. There were only two ways onto the Beach; by boat across the estuary, or on foot over the toll bridge to where, at its most western point, the Beach was joined to the mainland. This physical isolation suited both the inhabitants of Aduring itself and the inhabitants of the Beach. For the people who lived in bungalows on the Beach did not mix with the villagers of Aduring-by-Sea or Aduring Proper. Like all Aduring children, Tom had been warned to keep clear of the Beach people, just like country children were warned of gypsies who lay in wait for them in the wild woods, and city children were warned of the white slave traders lurking in dark alleyways by the docks.

'They're painted ladies, hussies, and Jack-the-lads,' his father had explained. 'From the music halls, theatres – and worse – so I've heard. Come down here at weekends to pursue their wicked ways, where they think the good Lord can't see them.' This information had only added to Tom's fascination and curiosity.

It was this part of Tom's world – Aduring Beach – to which the party from the London train was being steered in a small rowing-boat, that Sunday evening in June.

And although, of course, Tom had no way of knowing it, the arrival of this party at the Beach was about to change his world forever: that world which he took to be so small and fixed and frozen.

Indeed, not only change it, but turn it completely, frighteningly mad.

Chapter Three

'You makes a square. With your fingers and your thumbs . . .'

'Now what?'

'You look through it!'

Tom and his friend Ernest Afflick were stretched out on the riverbank, their stick and string fishing rods secured in a pair of forked hazel twigs. Tom and Ernest had been friends for as long as they could both remember. Ernest's people, like Tom's, were Primitive Methodists and as babies the two boys had been parked side by side in their perambulators in the chapel porch while their parents attended Sunday services. Since then, the arrival in the Afflick household over the years of four noisy and wearisome daughters, had caused Ernest to seek continuing refuge in Tom's company.

'You're bloomin' daft, Tom Jupe!' Ernest was swinging his head up and down, to and fro like a seaside telescope. 'What's the point of squinting through your fingers? You can only see bits of things.'

'It's making a photograph like . . .' Tom stopped and sighed inwardly. The excitement of framing an imaginary photograph was something he felt he couldn't explain. Perhaps Ernest saw the world differently. He did after all wear glasses. Small, thick lenses in thin wire frames.

'Give us a look through your specs, Ern.'

This was a familiar request, and Ernest slipped his glasses off his nose and handed them without a word to Tom.

The world through Ernest's glasses was bigger, but blurry. Great chunks of green and brown that were

14

hedgerows seemed to dance and to merge with chunks of grey that were the slate rooftops beyond. A sudden speckle of mottled colour caught Tom's eye.

'What's that?'

'Where?'

'Other side of the river. Past the railway bridge.'

'How do I know? You got my specs! Give 'em here . . .'

As soon as Tom handed Ernest back his glasses, the speckle became clearer to both of them. Two figures, a couple of hundred metres upstream, locked in a gentle embrace.

'Who is it, Tom?' Ernest's sight – even with his glasses on – wasn't quite good enough to make out the identity of either of the two lovers.

'Wilf Puttock.'

'Cor! 'Oo's his gal?'

'Er . . . can't quite make her out.' It was Maisie. Tom knew that, even though he couldn't see her face. He had seen her fixing that broad-brimmed straw hat earlier that morning. 'Goin' for a stroll with Annie Turk,' was what she had said as she left the cottage.

The young lovers did not look entirely at ease. Maisie, in a long white dress, clutched a parasol in her left hand and had a small handbag tucked under her elbow. Her right hand was preoccupied with adjusting her wide-brimmed hat which received a tidy blow from the peak of Wilf Puttock's cloth cap, every time he moved his face close to hers. He had placed a hand on each of Maisie's shoulders, so that he looked rather like a puppy begging for a biscuit.

Maisie – courting! And with Wilf Puttock! If his dad found out about Maisie and Wilf, then his chances of becoming an apprentice photographer would be gone forever, if indeed the chance was ever there anyway. Suddenly, the now familiar feeling of panic returned to Tom; the panic that was the vision of the future his father had mapped out for him.

'Ernest. What you goin' in for when you leave school?'

Ernest turned to Tom; surprised not just by the suddenness of his question, but also because it seemed to him to be a question that didn't really need asking. Tom's continued stare, though, begged a reply.

'Shop of course. What else?'

Ernest already helped his father in the family's small butcher's shop in Hope Street. His father had bought him a shining black delivery bicycle, which he pedalled furiously through the village on Saturday afternoons, delivering sausages, chops and Sunday joints. Ernest did not look a butcher's boy. He was thin and pale with sallow cheeks. Odd tufts of short, dullish-brown hair sprouted out at different angles from the top of his head. Looking at him, customers were automatically reminded of a scrag end of mutton, rather than of a nice, juicy shoulder of lamb; in short Ernest's appearance was not a good advertisement for the nutritional value of his father's meat.

'But don't you ever fancy doing something *different*, Ern?' There seemed just a touch of panic in Tom's voice.

'Not half! I fancy being an aeroplane flyer!'

Tom realised that his questions made as little sense to Ernest as did his friend's view of the world without a pair of glasses.

'Bloomin' 'eck!' Ernest's eyes were trained on Maisie and Wilf Puttock. The couple were a little further off now, on the side of the hedgerow that bordered the riverside path. Both were hatless, and even Ernest saw them sink out of sight below the hedge line.

'Cor. They're lyin' on the grass! Now that's what I call a spoon!' declared Ernest, with some excitement.

A train thundered by on the railway bridge above their heads.

'That's the Portsmouth slow. Ten to. Time we done with the fishing, Ern.'

In the small seaside village of Aduring-by-Sea, where kissing and cuddling was known as spooning and sitting about pondering the ways of the world was known as fishing, you could set your clocks by the slow train to Portsmouth.

The reason Tom and Ernest had to be done with their fishing was that it was Whit Monday. And for the congregation of the Prim, Whit Monday meant only one thing, the Bank Holiday Open Air Temperance Service: two hours of singing and sermons expounding the evils of drink, outside the wickedest, busiest public house in Aduring.

Silently, like an untidy battalion of infantrymen planning a surprise attack by stealth, they marched down Hope Street. Their destination was *The Jolly Sailor*, on the corner of Hope Street and Fore Street, the main road through Aduring, which ran parallel with the river. For this special occasion, the Prim congregation was augmented by other chapel-goers from the farms around Old Aduring, including Tom's grandparents, and by half a dozen Salvation Army bandsmen, their cornets and trumpets gleaming in the midday sun.

A few drinkers who were huddled outside the pub saw the dark mass approaching and scurried back into the crowded public bar where the noonday regulars screeched, roared and heaved in the low-ceilinged semi-darkness; shoving and elbowing their way sideways towards the bar itself, like stranded crabs desperate to reach the safety of the sea.

The Reverend Gilbert Comfort placed himself on the doorstep of *The Jolly Sailor* and gathered around him dark-stockinged girls and white-collared boys. Behind them, women in dark skirts that reached to the ground and men in even darker suits shuffled into place, spilling across the pavement and onto the street. All heads were covered; the women and girls wore wide-brimmed hats and bonnets, the men and boys caps and bowler hats.

Tom found it difficult to concentrate. He couldn't get out of his mind the picture of the hatless couple, arms entwined around each other, disappearing out of sight behind the riverside hedge. Could it really have been Maisie? He caught sight of her out of the corner of his eye; she was standing, hands folded demurely in front of her, listening to the elderly minister's words with an intent and serious expression, the very model of a decent chapel girl.

Drink, Mr Comfort was explaining, was the cause not only of all poverty, but of all the sins of the flesh. With his long, bony hands and his face as grey as the tablets of stone upon which God had inscribed the Ten Commandments, it seemed to Tom as if the minister had very little flesh left to sin with. He finished talking and held up his right arm. Immediately, the whole gathering burst into song:

> *Throw out a lifeline! Throw out a lifeline!*
> *Someone is sinking awa-y-y-y!*
> *Throw out a lifeline! Throw out a lifeline!*
> *Someone is sinking today!*

A woman stumbled out of the pub. She was wrapped in layers of filthy rags that hid any natural shape her body might have had. She looked as though she had spent the last week rolling around in the street – which she probably had. Her bright red hair stood out from her head at all angles, coarse and matted and her eyes blazed like the fires of hell. Ginger Jenny.

'Carn't you misser- misserububble ol' blighters shrrup! We carn't 'ear ourself drink in there!' She had no front teeth and great jets of spittle landed on the coat sleeve of the horror-struck minister, still trying to claim the front step of *The Jolly Sailor* as his pulpit. Ginger Jenny rocked uneasily and for one moment Tom thought she was going to fall, but she swung back upright again. She lurched and staggered down Fore Street and round the bend towards the harbour.

Rescue the perishing! Care for the dying!
Jesus is beckoning, Jesus can save!

Another Temperance hymn rattled windows and shook beer pots on the tables. As the Salvation Army Captain counted the beats between the chorus and the verse a dreadful scream pierced the air. Ginger Jenny came back into view, stumbling and panting towards them.

'No!' gasped Ginger Jenny, seizing Mr Comfort's wet sleeve and desperately trying to hide behind him. 'No! Dear Jesus, forgive me. It's coming for me, it's coming for me, a beast full of eyes before and behind!' she added, showing a commendable knowledge of the Revelations of St John.

If only I had a camera, thought Tom.

The minister was pushing at Ginger Jenny's shoulders, trying to shake her off, but her sharp nails were well able to grip his sleeve. By now, customers were tumbling out of *The Jolly Sailor*, blinking in the bright sunlight, cackling and roaring. The spectacle of a wrestling match between the Reverend Gilbert Comfort of the Primitive Methodist Chapel and Ginger Jenny promised to be far more entertaining than anything the public bar could provide.

The congregation shrank back into the road, as if they were afraid that the beery reek of Ginger Jenny's breath might somehow suffocate them. They did not bother to look in the direction of the harbour, being more concerned to keep out of Ginger Jenny's path.

Tom though, standing as he was with Ernest on the edge of the gathering, did see something out of the corner of his eye. He nudged his friend in the ribs.

'Bloomin' 'eck, Ernest!' Tom's panic-stricken voice was raised to fever pitch. 'It's a tiger! Run for it!'

As one, the Bank Holiday Open Air Temperance Service congregation looked up to see a huge, brightly-striped tiger pounding towards them on its hind legs.

Chapter Four

'**A**wroaghhhh!' roared the tiger.

'Jesus!' gasped *The Jolly Sailor*'s' customers in fearful alarm.

'Jesus!' gasped the Temperance Service congregation in prayerful panic.

The children in the Temperance congregation had been quick to shin up lamp-posts, climb drain pipes and clamber onto window-sills. Meanwhile, their adult counterparts turned and tried to run for it back up Hope Street, in the wake of Ginger Jenny's screams.

Squeezed onto a neighbouring window-sill, Tom and Ernest could see everything.

'Cor! There be trouble!' shouted Ernest, rubbing his glasses with undisguised glee. 'They ain't goin' to make it!'

Those *Jolly Sailor* customers who had made their way out onto the pavement to jeer at Ginger Jenny and Mr Comfort were the last to respond; their faculties being somewhat impaired by the effects of the very same demon drink that the minister had been warning them about. But even they had sensed the urgency of the situation and had turned to take refuge in the safest haven they knew – the public bar – where they had found their way blocked by fellow drinkers. So they, too, now tried to run back up the road.

'Out of the way, you lot!' yelled the tiger, in a rich bass voice.

'Blimey!' whistled Tom.

For Ginger Jenny, never steady on her feet at the best of times, suddenly tripped and fell. The fleeing Primitive Methodists could not avoid her; and the swaying drinkers from *The Jolly Sailor* could not avoid the stumbling Methodists. In an instant, saints and sinners lay scattered like skittles across the whole breadth of Hope Street.

And somewhere, in the midst of them all, Ginger Jenny.

'Out of the way you lot!' yelled the tiger again, as he ploughed into the sea of skirts and stays, swearing and sobbing.

'Get the old woman!' yelled a voice a little way off. Tom turned to see a trolley being pushed by two shirt-sleeved men. On the trolley was another man behind what appeared to be a large camera on a tripod. Running alongside the trolley was a large man in a Norfolk jacket. The same man who had arrived on the London train the evening before with a middle-aged woman, a young girl, two young men and a great deal of luggage.

'I'll get you! I'll get you!' roared the tiger, menacingly, burrowing for Ginger Jenny among the arms and legs of the petrified Prims.

Tom could just make out the dishevelled figure of his father, pulling his mother out of the mêlée.

'Steady, you chaps! Hold it there!' bellowed the man in the Norfolk jacket to the trolley-pushers.

'A beast full of eyes!' Ginger Jenny suddenly rolled out of the mêlée; like a rugby ball from a scrum. She swaggered unsteadily to her feet, but in her blind, drunken, frightened stupor ran the wrong way. Straight into the belly of the brightly-striped tiger.

'Oof! Gotcha!' said the tiger.

Ginger Jenny let out one last pitiful cry and then fell down in a dead faint at his feet.

Tom looked from Ginger Jenny to the tiger, to the cameraman, to the minister; then to his parents, who were struggling to their feet on the far side of the crowd. He could have done with twenty pairs of eyes.

'Marvellous, dear boy! Splendid!' The large man in the Norfolk jacket was hugging the cameraman.

'N-N-Not 'arf, Guv'nor! This one'll 'ave 'em creased up in their seats!' The cameraman's face shone like an angel's.

'You did it, Arthur, old thing!' the large man in the Norfolk jacket was shaking the tiger by its paw.

The tiger pulled off its head to reveal the actor beneath: an actor whose thick black hair, handsome face and bushy moustache were covered in sweat.

'You don't think this lot spoiled it?' he asked, jerking his head contemptuously at the fallen Primitive Methodists, for all the world as if they were a gang of meddling street urchins.

'Not a bit of it! They'll add mightily to the comic effect, mark my words!'

In truth, none of the members of the Temperance congregation was seriously hurt. The women's numerous layers of skirts, corsets and other undergarments ensured that minor bruising was the most serious injury sustained by any of them. The heavy use of the street by traffic during normal working days meant any fall was cushioned by a generous layer of horse manure.

The minister's wife, meanwhile, was administering smelling salts to the slowly recovering Ginger Jenny, while Mr Comfort himself, his thin hands shaking with anger, strode purposefully to the large man in the Norfolk jacket.

'How dare you, sir, intrude upon the preaching of the Word of God in such a disgraceful and dangerous manner!'

The large man in the Norfolk jacket did not appear to be particularly concerned by the minister's outburst. 'My dear vicar, if you insist on presuming that you have some God-given right to use the public highway as a pulpit –'

'I do not intend to be told by you where or where not

I should choose to preach the Word of God. Besides, many of the people here are elderly and frail. Serious injury could have occurred –'

'That's as may be, vicar, but nobody looks as though there's anything wrong with them that a tot of rum won't soon cure, eh? As a measure of good faith, please allow me to buy –'

'Sir. This is . . . was . . . the gathering of the Annual Aduring-by-Sea Bank Holiday Open Air *Temperance* Service!'

The large man in the Norfolk jacket burst out laughing. 'Temperance? My mistake, vicar! And my apologies! But listen, you and your flock should be proud of yourselves. You have, albeit unwittingly, taken part in a small slice of history today; for you have all had the good luck to find yourselves appearing in the very first moving picture to be made at Aduring-by-Sea by the South Seas Film Company!' He held out a podgy hand to the minister, who kept his fist firmly clenched.

'Luck?' he hissed, as if the man in the Norfolk jacket had just uttered the vilest blasphemy. 'There is no such word in my dictionary. Our actions are shaped by two hands only, the hand of the Lord and the hand of the Devil, and I have no doubt who is the guiding force behind your unseemly works.'

The South Seas Film Company, so that was who they were! Tom had half an eye on the large man in the Norfolk jacket and one and a half eyes on the splendid camera. The cameraman was making some adjustments to the lens and Tom was within a few metres of him, when a strong hand roughly grabbed his elbow.

'Home!' his father ordered. His chapel suit was uncharacteristically creased and dusty. His mother, her hat dented and awry, followed with Maisie, a few paces behind.

To avoid walking back through the dreadful scene, Mr

Jupe led his family right down Fore Street, then back up Nile Street, which ran parallel with Hope Street.

As they hurried by the back of *The Jolly Sailor*, Tom thought he could still hear the rich, lusty laughter of the large, jolly-faced man in the Norfolk jacket.

Chapter Five

'Who will Dare to Be a Daniel?'

Mr Comfort sat in the small and dimly-lit chapel vestry and addressed half a dozen Prim boys at mid-week Bible Class.

'Who Will Fight Against the Foe?'

He grabbed the curved wooden arms of his chair as if he fully expected them to turn into swords.

'Who Is on the Lord's Side? Who Will Serve the King?'

The old man drew a quick rattling breath and did not bother to await a reply.

'The Devil's work takes many forms. What then are we to make of his latest tool – kinemagraphics? It is not so much lions that Daniel has to face in the den, but *tigers*! A man dressed as a wild animal pursues a poor drunken wretch of a woman through a public thoroughfare and collides with a congregation of worshippers. Photographs are taken, which we are told can be made to move and these will be shown to members of the public! Such base and degrading vanities have their evil roots in the dark dens their begetters have suddenly sprung from – I mean, of course, the nation's theatres and playhouses. Why should people dress up as characters except to hide the sins of their own? Why should people seek the sham world of the playhouse and the theatre except to run away from the sin in themselves? But there is no hiding place from the Lord; neither are there any secrets from Him . . .'

Tom fidgeted uncomfortably as he found his own

thoughts getting in the way of the minister's words. Tom held no secrets from God, but he held a big secret from his parents, Maisie and even Ernest. And his secret was this: he could not stop thinking about the large man in the Norfolk jacket, and the fresh-faced young cameraman. He wanted more than anything to go to the Beach and seek these people out. They seemed so different from anyone he knew in Aduring. Even different from Wilf Puttock, who was the only person, Tom felt, who really understood his enthusiasm for photography.

But although the Beach was only a hundred metres across the harbour, in truth it was as far away as the jungles of central Africa.

It was no use Tom telling his parents he wanted to go across to the Beach for an afternoon, he knew that. The river, the meadows and hills beyond were open to Tom, but the Beach was the one place where he was forbidden to go. One might as well ask permission to go and take tea with the Devil himself.

It was no use lying to his parents; pretending he was going to spend an afternoon's fishing on the riverbank. You either rowed over to the Beach, or you took the one road, a rough track on the far end of the toll bridge over the river. It was impossible to get across there without being seen. And Tom had enough relatives in Aduring to guarantee that at least one nosy old aunt with nothing better to do all day than watch and gossip about 'goings on' would report his movements to his mother.

'Seen your Tom goin' over to the Beach last Sat'day,' one of his aunts would be bound to say to his mother after chapel.

Neither was it any use asking Ernest to cover for him, for most days after school, and most Saturdays he was helping delivering meat for his father.

The old familiar feeling of panic swept over Tom again

as he saw himself trapped in a world he didn't really care for.

'. . . and so boys, you can all be Daniels. You can all be heralds of the good news. And this is how.'

Mr Comfort picked up a large brown paper parcel from underneath his Bible. He unwrapped the package, took out a bundle of cheaply printed leaflets and handed them round the class.

'𝕽𝖊𝖘𝖎𝖘𝖙 𝖄𝖊 𝖙𝖍𝖊 𝕯𝖊𝖛𝖎𝖑, 𝖆𝖓𝖉 𝕳𝖊 𝖜𝖎𝖑𝖑 𝕱𝖑𝖊𝖊 𝖋𝖗𝖔𝖒 𝖄𝖔𝖚!' Tom read, the thick black print smudging his fingers.

'There are enough of these tracts to go to every home in Aduring.' The minister's eyes shone expectantly in the dim room. 'So, who will spread the Word?' He made it sound as if the tracts were to be plastered across the village, like butter on bread.

'I will!' piped up Ernest, breathlessly. 'I can do 'em on my bicycle when I deliver the meat!'

Percy Alcock and Bert Crump agreed to deliver tracts in Aduring Proper. The Histed brothers offered to do the harbour cottages. Mr Comfort's expectant gaze fell upon Tom.

'If there's tracts enough for every 'ouse in Aduring, does that mean the bungalows on the Beach 'as got to be done?' Tom asked the minister, quietly.

When Tom got home from Bible Class, he found his mother and Maisie were at the table darning socks in the light of the hissing oil lamp. Mr Jupe was at the table, writing a letter regarding chapel business in a long, careful hand.

'And what's the purpose of this lot?' Mrs Jupe pointed to Tom's armful of tracts.

'One to every 'ouse in Aduring. Mr Comfort's asked me to do far side of the toll bridge.'

' 'As he now?'

'Well, Ernest's always working in the shop now . . . It'd

give me something to do,' Tom added needlessly, guiltily by way of explanation.

His father and mother exchanged a brief glance.

'Well, I'm glad to see you have a will to do the Lord's work,' said his father.

Maisie looked up, suspiciously.

His mother sighed. 'Well, just you take care,' she threatened.

'I shall be just like Daniel goin' into the lions' den,' grinned Tom.

Mrs Jupe looked up sharply from her darning towards her son, and let out a small cry as her needle slipped and pierced the ball of her thumb.

'That's what Mr Comfort said,' added Tom, quickly.

The Lord, as the Reverend Gilbert Comfort might also have said, works in mysterious ways.

Chapter Six

Straight after school next day, Tom marched down
Fore Street, his parcel of tracts tucked under his arm.
He bade 'good afternoon' to Mr Amos Carp, leaning
against the door of the toll bridge cottage. Mr Carp it was
who spent his hours collecting pennies and ha'pennies
from the passing traffic. It was rumoured that Amos Carp
had never been out; that he stayed forever in his little
round cottage, like some twentieth-century troll.

The toll bridge itself supported massive stone arches at
each end, and through these Tom walked with his parcel of
tracts the next day after school on his way to the Beach. It
was like walking out of the safety of a castle keep and into
a new and dangerous world beyond.

Tom turned onto the rough track that took him straight
onto the Beach. Two long uneven lines of flimsy wooden
bungalows sat squat among the shingle on each side of the
road. Some of them were actually old railway carriages that
had been painted bright colours and hung with the frilliest
of net curtains. They looked rather awkward and forlorn,
Tom thought, as if they had been washed up there on the
shingle by some huge storm.

Tom had about three hundred tracts in a brown paper
bag. Not that he had bothered to stop to deliver any. He
was too busy looking for any building that could possibly
house the headquarters of the South Seas Film Company.
He did not know what a film company's headquarters
would actually look like, but Mr Comfort had mentioned
them in the same breath as theatres and music halls, so he
had formed the impression in his mind of a large brick

building fronted by tall columns, with huge notices pro-claiming SOUTH SEAS FILM COMPANY in large, bright letters.

It was with a sense of disbelief and despair that Tom realised he had almost reached the *end* of the Beach, where the old fort looked out across the mouth of the harbour towards France. The afternoon sun was hot and bright and Tom could see no one about. He remembered his father's words about the Beach people: 'They come down here at the weekends to pursue their wicked ways.' Perhaps nobody came to the Beach on weekdays.

'Lookin' for summon, boy?' A fisherman's head bobbed up from behind a small boat.

'Er . . . The South Seas Film Company?'

The fisherman grinned, displaying a full row of black teeth. He looked through Tom as if he could see all his guilty secrets and dreams.

'Down there.' The fisherman pointed a wiry finger straight at a large greenhouse, just a hundred metres from the water's edge.

Tom stared at it disbelievingly. He had been aware of it out of the corner of his eye, but had assumed that it was part of some kind of market garden, housing ripening tomatoes.

'What business ha' you wi' them then?'

Tom took out a tract from his paper bag.

'I'm deliverin' these.' He handed it to the fisherman who shook his head.

'It's no use to me, boy, I can't make no sense of writin'. What's it say?'

'Resist Ye the Devil, and He will Flee from You.'

'Mmm.' The fisherman nodded his rough head slowly. 'I'll mark thy words, boy,' he said.

'There's a lot more stuff in it about turnin' away from the ways of the world.'

The fisherman looked thoughtful and serious, as if the text Tom had just given him contained some secret code or clue.

'But I'd still tek care if you a-gooing down there, boy.' The fisherman sidled up closer to Tom, his weather-beaten face ever watchful.

Tom felt his Adam's apple slither down from his throat to the pit of his stomach. 'Why?'

'They'm a mighty queer folk. That's why. And we're gooin' to be in fr'a fine old' sea mis', late ron.'

Tom looked hard at the greenhouse and the sea beyond. Despite his apprehension, the rays of bright afternoon sunshine reflecting off the glass and the dull rhythm of the waves seemed to draw him; and he found himself stumbling across the deep shingle towards the huge glasshouse.

Once he was right close up to it, the glare from the glass became less intense. Suddenly he stopped. From within the open door, he could hear voices. Voices that seemed to be getting closer. Two men deep in conversation were making for the door. Years of Prim sermons had fostered in Tom an acute sense of right and wrong. He knew he was trespassing and he knew it was wrong. He had to avoid being seen.

Behind him was an old black-tarred, wooden-slatted boathouse. The door was ajar, and Tom leapt inside, panting heavily as if he'd just run ten miles.

In the thin shaft of dusty sunlight that pierced through the open door, Tom could just make out the outline of a few chairs and, at the back of the shed, half a dozen packing cases stacked high. It had the appearance of a laundry, for at one end of the shed hung a huge white sheet, while dangling from the rafters were clothes-lines to which were pegged not shirts and smalls, but bits of film.

The voices, bright and animated, grew closer.

In a second, Tom had squeezed behind the packing cases.

The boathouse flooded with light as the door opened wide.

'W-W-Welcome, old son, to our very own Bijou Cinema!'

Tom was sure he recognised the voice as belonging to the cameraman he had seen on the trolley at the Temperance Service.

The other voice laughed. Tom dared not peep, for fear the voices would be looking his way. There was much murmuring and cursing. Then a match was struck.

'Okay. She's lit. P-P-Put the wood in the 'ole, and then we can roll!'

Pitch black, apart from a small, intense glow of a gas lamp.

A clanging, a whirring.

Tom peered out from his hiding place in the safety of the darkness. The two men sat each side of a card table in the middle of the room. On the table was a wooden box, resembling a large camera. Behind the box glowed a gas lamp, which the box itself seemed to magnify onto the white screen at the far side of the boathouse. The cameraman began to crank a handle on the side of the box. Large black blobs darted madly across the screen like giant ants scurrying for cover.

And then, Tom saw a giant photograph some two-metres square – a photograph which began to move.

Chapter Seven

Blurred and indistinct at first, then clearer and sharper, two small figures jerked and jolted their way across the screen. Peering out from the darkness at the back of the boathouse, Tom strained his eyes to make sense of the images. A wild animal seemed to be chasing an old lady through a village street.

Suddenly the images, like the pieces of a jigsaw, fell into place. The street was Fore Street; the wild animal, a tiger; the old lady, Ginger Jenny! There was a swift change of direction and the screen was full of dancing figures. Two boys on a window-sill appeared and were gone . . . Ernest and him? The scene outside *The Jolly Sailor* flashed before his eyes in the darkness like a silent dream.

The room brightened. More scurrying ants darted fitfully across the screen, which then turned brilliant white.

The cameraman stopped cranking the handle and his companion burst into applause. It was all Tom could do to stop himself joining him.

'T-T-Top 'ole, eh old man?' asked the cameraman.

'I should say so, Joe.'

'Now all we need is the titles!'

Joe turned off the gas lamp; then struck a match, and in the flickering light the two of them made for the door.

Sunlight streamed into the boathouse. The door was open enabling Tom to see not just the projector through which the moving pictures had been shown, but the camera and tripod still bolted to the trolley that had been pushed up Hope Street on Bank Holiday Monday.

Tom tip-toed across to the camera. It looked to be little more than a dark wooden box about the size of a biscuit tin. At one end was a brass rimmed lens and at the other a viewfinder. Still clutching his parcel of tracts, Tom leant forward and squinted into the viewfinder. The picture he saw was not a particularly interesting one, for the lens was pointing directly at the white screen. The only other object to fall within its frame was a tatty bentwood chair.

Tom could feel the cold metal of the rim of the viewfinder pressing against his cheek. As he blinked, the picture blurred – and became clear again.

And then the picture began to move.

A figure seemed to be walking towards him. A girl; her dark profile clear against the white screen. Calf-length dress and pinafore; dark stockings, loose auburn hair. Closer and closer she came, filling the viewfinder with her silent form.

Tom's heart thumped loud and hard. For a moment he couldn't think straight. Was he dreaming; or was he watching another moving picture? The girl was looking at him through the lens. Tom pulled away.

The girl remained.

She stood perfectly still. She had the darkest eyes Tom had ever seen. There was something rather sad and faraway about them. They seem too old for her somehow, Tom thought, for she couldn't have been much older than him.

'I'm Laura,' she said. 'I expect you want Father. He's over in the bungalow. Come on.'

With a slight toss of the head, she turned and walked towards the door.

Tom needed no second bidding. He passed his parcel of tracts from one hand to the other, then instinctively realising that they could be the source of severe embarrassment for him, he looked round for somewhere to hide them. There was a large empty tin box by his feet. Without further thought, Tom popped his tracts in and closed the lid.

Then he ran out of the boathouse after the dark-eyed girl.

Laura's father's bungalow was only a few metres away from the boathouse, on the other river side of the road. It was larger than the railway carriage bungalows, and built entirely from weatherboard; painted cream, with bright green window frames.

'Come on,' said Laura again, as Tom searched in vain for a doormat on which to wipe his boots. He followed her into the sitting room.

It was a room the like of which Tom had never seen before. It seemed big enough to play a football match in, full of light and space. Brightly-coloured rugs were scattered on the floor. The matchwood walls were painted white and on them hung photographs of men and women in all sorts of costumes. By contrast, the Jupes' living room was not big enough to swing a skipping rope in; Tom knew this because once, when he was younger Maisie and her friend Letty had tried it and had ended up knocking the framed text 𝕲𝖔𝖉 𝖎𝖘 𝖙𝖍𝖊 𝕳𝖊𝖆𝖉 𝖔𝖋 𝕿𝖍𝖎𝖘 𝕳𝖔𝖚𝖘𝖊 off the wall, completely shattering the glass. The Jupes' living room was also packed with chairs, tables, two sideboards and a dresser. (Their front room was equally crowded, but was only used for important visitors, like the minister or Great-Aunt Fanny from Hove.) The entire contents of this room, though, consisted of two wicker armchairs, a chaise longue and, in the corner, a roll-top desk at which sat a large man in a brightly-coloured Paisley waistcoat.

Laura went up and rapped this gentleman on the head sharply with her knuckles.

'Rat-tat-tat!' she said.

'Who is that?'

'Two fleas dancing under your hat!'

The man roared with laughter and spun round. Tom recognised him immediately as the large, jolly-faced man who had introduced himself to Mr Comfort as the manager of the South Seas Film Company.

'I've found a boy, Barney.'

Tom winced. He hated the way she sounded as if she'd brought her father a bit of old driftwood off the beach. And he hated being described as a *boy*; he felt much older than that. And if this was Laura's father, why did she call him Barney?

'Mmm, yes, I can see that. Sit down, dear boy, sit down do. You'll wear the pattern off the rug shuffling about like that. You'll take a little cawfy with us, of course? Of course! Laura, fetch another cup for our visitor.' Tom had never drunk coffee in his life. He seemed to recall his father talking about it in much the same way as he talked about gambling, Sunday newspapers and 'that sort of woman'.

'I receive two kinds of enquiry here,' Laura's father continued, 'those pertaining to positions and those pertaining to . . .' his booming descended to a whisper, '. . . money. Judging by the youthfulness of your years and the manner of your bearing, I would guess that your particular enquiry relates to positions.'

An extravagant man by nature, the manager of the South Seas Film Company would never use one short, sharp word, where twenty long, flowing ones were freely available. Tom, meanwhile, found his head too full to reply.

'He wants to be a cameraman.' Laura handed her father a cup.

Tom's cheeks burnt bright red. What did *she* know?

'Wise man, wise man indeed! A good cameraman is worth a dozen half decent actors.' Laura's father poured the coffee from the silver jug. 'Black or white?'

Tom's cheeks burnt more fiercely still. What did this all

mean? What was a black cameraman? What was a white cameraman? But Laura saw his agonised stare and came to his rescue.

'Your coffee. Do you take it with milk, or without?'

'Er . . . Without. Please,' muttered Tom, praying for all he was worth that he had said the right thing.

'And what exactly, dear boy, is your present position?'

The fires in Tom's cheeks were stoked again.

'Er . . . I'm still at school like . . . But I'm done next summer. Easter if I get apprenticed . . .' His voice trailed off.

'School eh?' Laura's father sounded intrigued, as if Tom had told him he was an Arctic explorer or a designer of flying machines. 'Never been to a school myself. Far too busy for that sort of thing. Is it an interesting sort of life? Being a scholar?'

Tom thought of the hours spent in the schoolroom, squashed onto his hard, wooden bench, hunched over his slate, counting the long seconds to the end of the day.

'No. Not really.'

Laura's father shook his head sadly. 'I've heard much the same kind of reports from other fellows who've been to school.' Suddenly he jumped, as if he'd been bitten on the bottom by a bee. 'Heavens above, dear boy, here we are gossiping away like two old stagers in a dressing-room and I don't even know what they call you!'

'My name's T–' Tom stopped. If he told them his real name, it would only take a chance word in the village for everything to come out. And Tom could see that Laura's father was a man of very many words. If his parents found out that instead of spreading the Word amongst the heathen and sinners, he was now taking coffee with them, there would be trouble, of that he was sure.

Somewhere inside him, he was still deeply afraid of these people whom everybody he knew had warned him against, whom the fisherman had called 'mighty queer folk'. He was after all, Mr Comfort had said, 'like Daniel going into the lions' den'. Some irrational notion seemed to tell him that if these people didn't know who he really was; if they didn't know his real name, he would be safe.

'Er . . .' Tom's brain found a new gear. 'My name's Daniel,' he declared, boldly. 'Daniel Lyons.'

Chapter Eight

Laura's father rammed his thumbs into the pockets of his waistcoat.

'You know who I am, of course!'

All Tom knew was that the man was Laura's father and that he was presumably something to do with the South Seas Film Company. Again, Laura, sitting on her father's desk, swinging her legs, saw Tom's embarrassment in his lack of reply.

'Honestly, Barney, sometimes you are just too pompous! Why *should* he know who you are? This isn't Hammersmith!'

Laura slipped down from the desk, strode halfway across the room towards Tom, bowed and thrusting out an arm towards her father fixed Tom with a dark-eyed stare.

'May I present, the one, the only, Mr Barnaby Merry, General Manager of the Alhambra Theatre, Hammersmith and Sole Proprietor of The South Seas Film Company, Aduring-by-Sea!'

Mr Barnaby Merry smiled, stood up and took a bow. Laura clapped furiously and Tom, though he felt extremely silly about it, attempted to do the same.

'If we have all done with our cawfy, perhaps we should show Daniel the studio, eh?' announced Mr Merry.

As soon as they stepped inside the great glasshouse, a stifling blast of heat took Tom's breath away.

'Put a potato on the floor in here just after breakfast and it'll be baked in time for luncheon,' said Mr Merry.

They seemed to be in the hall of a great country mansion. A huge wooden staircase wound upwards before them. Tom looked up and saw that upstairs it fanned out to the left and to the right, but led . . . nowhere!

'*The Horror at Hatherwick Hall*.' Mr Merry winked and raised a knowing eyebrow. 'Last week, though, it was Blackamour Castle, for' – and he put on a blood-curdling voice – '*The 'And That 'Aunted 'Er.*'

They walked through a door at the back of the 'hall' and came out into a filthy scullery. Tom's eyes roved over a cobwebbed window and a broken stone sink, caked with mud and dirt. Then they fixed on the object that was lying in the sink.

A hand.

Large and pink, with long, claw-like nails.

Tom felt rather sick and dizzy.

'What's that doing here?' asked Laura. She picked up the hand and threw it at Tom, who jumped back two paces.

'It's only a dummy hand,' she giggled.

Roaring with laughter Mr Merry picked up the hand and pulling a couple of wires at the wrist made the fingers move. Tom shivered.

'This, dear boy, is the very 'And That 'Aunted 'Er; in our little film we made last week, don't you see? And this –' he flung out his arms in an expansive gesture, '– this is Bob Cratchit's cottage. *A Christmas Carol*.'

They made their way around the back of a grey oilcloth wall and into a ladies' boudoir. Rich drapes hung from the walls and a peach-coloured silk coverlet was spread across the bed.

'That's from Ma's bedroom!' Laura sounded horrified.

'She won't mind,' said Mr Merry, quickly, but uncertainly, 'once she realises it's for the good of the Company.'

He winked at Tom. '*The Ruin Of Them All*,' he explained.

They walked out of the boudoir and into an empty greenhouse.

'We'll be building sets here, too, later on,' Mr Merry went on. 'Twenty films I plan to have completed by the end of the summer. Comedy, tragedy, melodrama, there's nothing Barnaby Merry won't try! We're going to turn the boathouse into a cinema, so that the people of Aduring can come across the bridge and see the fruits of our labours! "The Bijou", I'm going to call it!'

'G-G-Guv'nor!' a voice behind them called. Tom recognised the cameraman.

'Joe! Did you get young Arthur off all right?'

'P-P-Put him into a third-class carriage jest in time,' grinned Joe.

'This is Daniel, who wants to be a cameraman, by the way.'

Joe held out his hand and Tom took it. Joe pumped Tom's hand up an down like a piston. 'It's c-c-certainly the life, Dan; it's c-c-certainly the life!' He turned to Mr Merry. 'He roared at *Mother's Ruin*, Guv'nor, blinkin' roared!'

'*Mother's Ruin* is our very first film, Daniel. We were out in Aduring Bank Holiday trying out our new camera. Young Arthur Schwartz was down – he does a bit of acting for us, so we decked him out in our tiger's costume, the idea being it was a film about a circus, do you follow me?'

Tom nodded.

'Then this old dame, much the worse for drink, spots us and screams blue murder, because she thinks Arthur's a *real* tiger! So we follow hot foot and the faster we follow, the louder she screams. And then d'you know what?'

Tom did know, but he shook his head.

'We turn a bend and career straight into one of these dreadful holier-than-thou prayer meetings! What a piece of luck! So our adventure about a circus turns into a comedy about drink – *Mother's Ruin!*'

Laura, Joe and Mr Merry were all helpless with laughter. Tom smiled.

'M-M-Mind you, we shouldn't laugh, Guv'nor. Look what happened to old Cronin at the London and Britannia – he actually found a bunch of these Bible-bashers singing hymns outside his studio one day!'

The four of them made their way out of the great glass studio and down to the sea's edge. The water sucked quietly at the shingle, for there was hardly any whiff of a breeze. The sun was fading fast, too fast; Tom knew that the fisherman had been right; a sea mist was on its way.

Tom looked at Joe and saw that he, like Mr Merry and Laura, was staring silently out to sea.

'The light here's jes' p-p-perfect,' stammered Joe. 'And the air's so bright and clean. We could never get the same effect if we made our films in London.'

'It's a truly beautiful spot.' Mr Merry spoke in a voice barely above a whisper.

They stood in silence a moment longer, then, 'When are you making another film?' asked Tom.

'Saturday week – all being well. Can't get my actors down 'til then. Theatre commitments. I try to tell 'em the future's all in films, but they won't listen. We're not mime artistes, they say. They don't like not being able to make all their speeches, you see, Daniel.'

'You must come,' Laura said.

'Not 'arf!' added Joe.

'There'll certainly be plenty for you to do,' agreed Mr Merry. 'I can always do with a utility man – if you can get away, that is . . .'

Mr Merry's words brought Tom up with a start. His parents! They would have been expecting him back ages ago. He struggled to his feet.

'I got to go now. Thank you for the cawfy.'

'Our pleasure, dear boy. Hope to see you Saturday week.'

'T-T-Top 'ole,' added Joe.

''Bye . . .'

Tom staggered up the shingle to the top of the beach. Ahead of him lay the Merrys' bungalow and beyond it a few fishing boats resting in the grey, rippling river. But on the far side of the estuary, the chimney skyline of the quay and the great square tower of St. Cosmo's Church behind them were already being swallowed up into the mist.

'Daniel! Daniel!'

It took a few seconds for Tom to realise it was he who was being called. He turned and saw Laura just a few paces behind him.

'You *will* come, won't you? Saturday week.' She made it sound important.

''Course I will! I'll be comin'!' He was certain, even if he didn't know how. The fear and apprehension he had felt when he first set foot on the Beach had completely gone.

Laura turned and ran back into the bungalow and Tom began to sprint back along the track to the end of the Beach.

By the time he reached the broad stone arches that spanned the toll bridge, the bungalows on the Beach had disappeared into the mist as quickly as if they had been pictures on a screen.

Even the razor sharp eyes of Mr Carp in the toll cottage were hard put to identify the dim figure pounding over the river towards Aduring.

Chapter Nine

Tom had turned off Hope Street and into the twitten before he remembered that he had left his tracts in the boathouse.

He squeezed the latch on the back door of the cottage and crept into the scullery. The sound of unaccompanied singing floated through from the living room. Grace was being sung. Tom rinsed his hands in the sink, then turned and waited at the living room door for the singing to finish.

Be present at our table, Lord,
Be present here and ever more.

All was now quiet, but Tom still did not strike the latch. Then –

A-a-a-a-men.

Tom heard a faint rustle of skirts as his mother and sister sat down. It was the right moment to enter.

In the dim light Tom could make out the grey shadows of his parents and sister at the supper table. His father was slicing pieces off what smelt to Tom like bacon pudding. Without looking up his father said:

'Are your hands washed?'

'Yes, Dad.'

'Supper is at seven o'clock in this house. Not at five past seven.'

'Yes, Dad. I'm sorry I'm late. I sort of lost track of the time, like . . .'

'Say your own grace.'

Tom placed both hands on the back of his chair and closed his eyes.

'Di dum di dum di dum . . .' he said to himself as his mind filled with images of greenhouses, black-toothed fishermen, Paisley waistcoats, smiles, looks and the gently sucking sea.

'Amen.'

Tom's mother passed him a plate of bacon pudding.

'How d'you get on then, boy?'

'With the tracts?'

'What else?'

'I delivered 'em, all right.'

'All of 'em?' Maisie exclaimed, incredulously.

'Yes,' said Tom truthfully, not bothering to add that every single one had been delivered into a tin box in what was soon to become the 'Bijou Cinema'.

'Well, it's certainly brought a bit of colour to his cheeks,' said his mother.

'I been running, ain't I?' explained Tom, feeling very hot and flustered.

'See anyone?'

'See Mr Carp,' said Tom truthfully, not bothering to add that he had seen various members of the South Seas Film Company as well.

'Eat up, boy,' said his father.

And there ended the first inquisition.

The school playground was buzzing. Groups of children huddled under the classroom windows, by the great oak door and round the back of the toilets. There was only one topic of conversation.

'They'm making fillums.'

'Gooin' to show 'em over on the Beach like.'

'Aren't!'

'Are, so there. I seen posters.'

'My sister what's in service in Lunnon, she been and she say they do put all the lights out!'

At this revelation, there were shrieks of excitement from the girls and puzzled frowns from the boys.

'It's jest tricks. Can't see nurthin'. They'm jester blur.'

'Aren't!'

'Are! I paid a 'apenny to see one at the fun fair last year.'

'These films are proper!' Tom could keep silent no longer. 'You can make out people's faces and that!'

'What d'you know, Tom Jupe?'

'Yeh, what d'you know?'

'I've seen the film already!' he wanted to say. 'And I've taken cawfy with Mr Barnaby Merry, and I'm goin' to help 'em make films,' but he dared not.

Instead – 'That's what I've heard, anyway,' he retorted, lamely.

'Prims don't know nurthin'!'

Which, to a great extent – at least when it came to worldly things like films – was true. Very simple films, no more than a minute long, had been a common part of fairground attractions for the last few years. London and large towns like Brighton already had small cinemas, but members of the Prim did not frequent such dens of iniquity.

For Tom, the great glass studio seemed a world away and Saturday week even further.

> *There is a Happy Land*
> *Far, far away.*
> *Where saints in Glory stand!*
> *Bright, bright as day.*
> *Oh! We shall Happy be!*
> *When from sin and sorrow free,*
> *There in our Happy Land!*
> *Far, far away.*

At Sunday morning service in the Primitive Methodist chapel, no one sang more lustily than Tom Jupe; no one prayed harder than Tom Jupe; no one listened to the sermon more intently than Tom Jupe.

'In my Father's house are many mansions . . .' the minister quoted the vision of heaven according to the Gospel of St. John.

And Tom saw a great glasshouse, filled with haunted hallways, filthy sculleries and luxurious boudoirs, in which there dwelt laughing men in bright, Paisley waistcoats and dark-eyed, smiling girls with painted faces. A Happy Land. Across the estuary. Far, far away.

Chapter Ten

It came as a shock to Tom to realise just how easy it was to lie to his parents.

'I'm goin' fishin' today – that all right?'

'With Ernest?'

'No, 'e's out deliverin' for the shop. No, I mean on my own like. I thought I'd go for the day.'

'For the day?' spluttered Maisie, her mouth full of hatpins. Tom shot her a brief glare and she quickly, almost apologetically, turned away. Not like Maisie at all. Did she suspect that he knew about her and Wilf Puttock, perhaps?

'I want to go up river.'

Mr Jupe stroked his spiky moustache. 'Well, it's certainly the weather for it, boy.'

The sun was already bright in the early morning sky.

'You better take a piece o' pie, if you're goin' to be out all day!' his mother called from the scullery.

If any of Tom's nosy aunts had been peeking from behind their heavy front room curtains or even been standing by shop doorways gossiping in bitter tones about who had done what with whom and when and what was the world coming to, they would have seen their young nephew stepping out along Fore Street towards the toll bridge, fishing rod in hand. But they would not have seen him drop his rod off in a clump of bushes at the roadside on the far side of the bridge. Nor would they have seen him break into a jog up the track that led to the Beach, rather than cross the meadow that led down to the river's edge.

Tom could hear the shouting and clatter and laughter

almost as soon as he set foot on the Beach road. By the time he drew level with the Merrys' bungalow, he could see that the Beach had changed from the quiet, almost eerie secret place that he had visited ten days before, to a noisy, busy place of work.

The door of the great glass studio was open. In ran a shirt-sleeved young man carrying a table; out rushed another shirt-sleeved young man carrying a chair. In ran a young man carrying three long planks of wood; out rushed another young man carrying six short planks of wood. Just outside the door, a woman in a nightgown was arguing with a frock-coated butler. A little way from the studio, a policeman was standing on his head, singing. No one took the slightest notice of Tom, who hung about forlornly, clutching his slice of pork pie.

'Hey!'

Tom turned to find himself facing a young man with a rifle.

'You busy?'

Tom shook his head.

'Take this in to Bruno, would you?'

'Right . . .' said Tom, stuffing his pork pie into his jacket pocket.

The studio was sizzling like an oven, even though the morning outside was still fresh.

In front of the *Hatherwick Hall* grand staircase, was the camera on its tripod, and in front of the camera, squinting between his forefingers and thumbs was Joe.

'T-T-Top 'ole, old chap! You don't need a rifle to shoot a film, you know!' and he burst into a long chortle.

'Someone told me to give it to Bruno.'

'Over by the grandfather clock. He's the wicked Baron.'

Bruno was almost as tall as the grandfather clock and twice as broad.

'Theese? Theese my gun? There iss nothing beeger?' Bruno looked down at Tom with incredulous contempt. In his great hands, the gun looked no bigger than a child's water pistol.

Then Mr Barnaby Merry himself entered the studio. He wore a black bowler hat, a bow tie and, of course, a Paisley waistcoat. His sleeves were pulled halfway up his forearms by a pair of silver armbands. Round his neck there dangled a white cord, which disappeared into the depths of his waistcoat pocket.

'Five minutes!' he boomed. Then spotted Tom. 'Daniel, dear boy! Good to have you with us! You know our leading lady, of course . . .'

Just behind Mr Merry stood a girl whose short hair, rouged cheeks, scarlet lips and ankle-length white dress were unfamiliar, but whose dark brown eyes were not.

'Hello, Dan,' said Laura.

'I shoot her with theese . . . toy, huh?' Bruno angrily waved his rifle at Laura, as if he were a city gent waving a walking-stick.

'You shoot her from the depths of your black, black heart, Bruno, remember?' implored Mr Merry. 'It is Bruno Hoogenstadt the actor who will carry the scene, not Bruno Hoogenstadt the marksman.'

'Ah yees, ze black, black 'art!' And Bruno slunk off to the corner, caressing the rifle.

'He's such a sensitive boy,' sighed Mr Merry.

Tom didn't know whether the sweat on his forehead was the result of heat, fear or excitement. He found himself staring at Laura. She smiled. 'I'm the wicked Baron's step-daughter,' she explained.

Tom wiggled his head in a half-nod; his stiff, white collar already beginning to cut painfully into his neck.

'I'd take your coat and collar off if I were you, you look dreadfully hot.'

'Yes . . .' stammered Tom. He felt himself blush and that made him hotter still. He had never taken his coat and collar off in public before.

'Leave them by the door, they won't be in the way there.'

Tom removed his coat and collar, then rolled up his sleeves. He left his cap on, though.

'Scene one positions, everybody,' instructed Mr Merry, his arm raised high above his head.

'I have to go,' grinned Laura, making towards the staircase with the same little skip that Tom remembered from their first meeting in the boathouse.

Still with one arm raised, Mr Merry fished about in his waistcoat pocket and drew out a bright silver whistle which was attached to the cord around his neck. He gave three long blasts, then dropped his arm like a railway guard waving off a train.

Joe cranked a handle on the side of the camera, and the actors began to move.

In *The Horror at Hatherwick Hall*, the Baron's step-daughter slaved for him night and day –

'Whoa!' cried Mr Merry, as if he were dealing with a stubborn horse. Joe moved his camera so that it was pointing at the door.

The gallant young Count Peter – Joe's friend Arthur, minus tigerskin – came visiting. The Count immediately fell in love with the Baron's step-daughter, and the Baron banned him from the house. The step-daughter tried to escape and the Baron shot her. As she slumped onto the stairs, clutching her arm (fortunately it was only a flesh wound) –

'Whoa!' cried Mr Merry and Joe bounded up the stairs to get a few shots of the pain and anguish on the step-daughter's face. Then he bounded down the stairs again and there were three more blasts on the whistle from Mr Merry, as this time the Count bounded up the stairs to save the step-daughter. The wicked step-father made a desperate effort to stop his step-daughter and the Count from getting away.

Tom held his breath as the Baron toppled on the upstairs banister. Surely, if Bruno fell, he would be killed! Suddenly, with a great flourish, the Baron dropped over the banisters to the floor below. Tom felt his throat go dry but almost immediately there was a huge cheer from everyone in the studio.

'C-Come on, Dan! We need a hand with this bit!'

Tom followed Joe to where Bruno had fallen. He had landed on two mattresses, which of course had been out of the camera's view.

'H-H-Help us shift these.'

'I wass vair good, no?' asked Bruno.

'Very good,' said Tom, and he meant it.

Joe set up the camera under the balcony. The Baron lay prostrate on the floor. His step-daughter, tears streaming down her face, cradled his head in her arms, while the Count repeatedly struck his forehead with his hand. The Baron died, and the step-daughter fainted into the Count's arms.

Another huge cheer went up.

'Lovely! Lovely!' boomed Mr Merry.

'B-B-Bloomin' hunky dory, Guv'nor,' yelled Joe. 'What did you reckon, Daniel?'

Tom agreed. 'Bloomin' hunky dory,' he said, nodding furiously.

Laura's eyes were still wet with tears. She saw Tom's look of concern.

'It's all right,' she said laughing, 'they're not real! I used to need an onion, but I can bring them on whenever I like now.'

'Luncheon!' boomed Mr Merry.

'Must go and get out of this lot,' giggled Laura, scratching a rouge and crocodile tear-stained cheek.

Tom watched her skip off towards the bungalow and with a quiver of excitement suddenly realised that Laura was what his father would have called a 'painted lady'.

Chapter Eleven

here was a stiff salt breeze blowing off the sea. Joe and Tom sat at the water's edge, focusing – between forefingers and thumbs – on a lugger that was bobbing up and down half a mile out.

'Divide your frame into nine little boxes.'

'Eh?'

'In your head, old chap! Two lines down, two lines across. The corners of your middle box, they're the strong points in a picture. That's where your eye is drawn to. So that's where you put your subject.'

'Eh?'

'The fishing boat, old chap! That's your subject.'

Tom carefully placed the fishing boat in the bottom right-hand corner of his middle box.

'Every photographer has to know that.'

'Joe!' Arthur came running up, waving a newspaper. 'This morning's late edition! The London and Britannia burnt down last night!'

Joe scanned the newspaper report furtively. 'It says the most likely cause would appear to be accidental combustion.'

'Huh! Arson. It has to be. Try reading between the lines!' Arthur sloped off back up the Beach. Joe knitted his brows over the lines of tiny print.

'Why would someone burn down a film studio?' asked Tom, puzzled, and also a little frightened by Joe's serious countenance.

'B-B-Because, Tom old boy, there's quite a lot o' money

to be made out of this film business. Trouble is, some people don't have too many scruples about how they get their greedy mitts on it. Look at it this way, if you've got – say – ten companies making and selling films to the cinemas, the money's going to split ten ways; but if you've only got one company making films, then the money –'

'Won't need to be split at all.'

'You got the gist of it, old boy. So one or two of the bigger fish are arranging for some of the smaller companies to be smashed. Oh, they don't do it themselves. Oh no. They hire thugs called "busters" to do it for 'em.'

Tom shifted uneasily. Suddenly, in his mind, this new world of his, this world of fun and laughter, magic and mayhem seemed to have lost just a little of its sparkle; to have become just a little fragile.

'Guv'nor won't like it,' mused Joe, tucking the newspaper under his arm.

A whistle blast pierced the air. 'Two minutes!' Mr Merry's voice boomed from the studio door.

Joe got to his feet and stumbled back up the shingle to the studio. Tom turned and followed.

'Daniel!'

Tom looked up, sure now of his other name, sure now of the voice that was calling him. Laura was now back in her frock and pinafore, looking just like any other girl out of standard six, the top class at school. A tall woman, wrapped in a pale floral dress something like a bath robe, stood by her. Tom knew from her dark eyes that she must be Laura's mother.

'This is Daniel, Ma. He's going to be a cameraman with Joe.'

Mrs Merry held out her hand. 'Then I expect we'll be seeing quite a bit of you, Daniel.'

'I'm going up to the stores,' Laura announced. One of the railway carriage bungalows at the Aduring end of the

Beach was a kind of village shop and called itself 'Beach Stores'. It opened on Fridays and Saturdays when the Beach folk came down from London.

'Aren't you in no more films today then?'

'It's *Christmas Carol* this afternoon. I'm not in that.'

'*A Christmas Carol*? In July?'

'Yes, they've all got to stand around in that oven of a studio and shiver with cold, up to their ankles in cotton wool snow.' Nothing in this world was ever quite real, Tom thought.

'Are you coming, then?' Laura was swinging a wicker shopping basket to and fro, impatiently.

'I expect Daniel wants to watch the filming, Laura.'

Tom shrugged.

'I know!' said Laura excitedly, as they came out of the stores. For a dreadful moment, Tom thought she was going to suggest that they should go into Aduring. 'Let's walk back along through the sea.'

'Don't be silly. We'll get wet.'

'Not if we take our boots off!'

And for the first time since he had met her, Tom felt older than Laura. The sea had long lost its fascination for him as a playground. Walking along its edge was something he'd not done for years.

'Come on!' Laura already had her boots and stockings off and was racing over the shingle. Tom pulled off his boots and socks and ran after her. The hard pebbles made his toes curl up.

'It really pulls at your ankles!' called Laura.

They ran on until they reached a breakwater. Laura sat down beside it, hugging her knees. Tom mooched about at the water's edge, trying to skim pebbles across the waves.

After a bit, Laura said: 'You're really lucky living here.'

'What do you mean, lucky?'

'By the sea.'

'Don't you think you're lucky then? Being an actress and all that?'

'I don't think about it really.'

'I don't really think 'bout livin' by the sea.'

There was a long silence while they watched the foamy rivulets of the incoming tide race up the shingle, then slowly get drawn back again.

'You left school?' It seemed to Tom a more tactful way of finding out Laura's age, rather than asking her directly.

'Yes. I suppose so . . . I'm turned fourteen at any rate. Not that I ever really went to school.'

'No?'

'We were travelling most of the time. Different theatres and that. Ma and Barney taught me and other people in the company. I picked most things up myself. Once or twice I went; in London, when the School Board man caught up with us. But I never went for long.' Laura studied her toes for a bit. 'Not long enough ever to make any friends, anyway,' she added, wistfully.

'Why do you call your dad Barney?'

Laura laughed. 'When I was little I couldn't manage his name properly – Barnaby.'

'Yes, but why don't you call him Father or Pa? No one else I know calls their parents by their Christian names. You don't call your mother by her Christian name, do you? You call her Ma.'

'It's Elsie!' Laura broke into sudden peals of laughter. Tom found himself joining in, though he didn't really think Elsie was that funny a name; he had an Aunt Elsie.

'She hates it. She won't let anyone call her Elsie.'

'What about your father? What does he call her? Mrs Merry?' It was Tom's turn to laugh.

Laura nodded. 'He does! Sometimes. "Is that you Mrs

Merry?" he'll say, if she's just come in.' She mimicked her father's booming voice. 'Sometimes he calls her "my dear". Sometimes he calls her "my Notting Hill Nightingale".'

'My Notting Hill Nightingale?'

'That's her stage billing. Miss Adelaide Dupre, the Notting Hill Nightingale. You must have heard of her. She's much more famous than Barney.'

Pictures of the huge billboard on the side of the station flashed through Tom's mind. Huge red letters advertising forthcoming attractions at the Brighton Hippodrome. Vesta Tilley . . . Charlie Chaplin . . . Miss Adelaide Dupre, the Notting Hill Nightingale.

'I was called Little Jenny Wren. When I was about seven that was. I went on stage with Ma – Miss Adelaide Dupre the Notting Hill Nightingale and her Little Jenny Wren.'

'What are you called now?' asked a bemused Tom.

'Lorrilee Dupre. Barney thought it up. He said the Lorrilee was unique and the Dupre would trade on Ma's stage name.'

Laura picked up a smallish sharp-edged pebble and began carving in the soft wet wood of the breakwater.

'What are you doin' of?' asked Tom.

'Carving my name,' replied Laura.

'Oh yes? Which one?'

Laura ignored his question, but carried on carving. Tom began carving his name on the next breakwater up.

'What are *your* parents like, Daniel?'

Tom began digging among the pebbles, furiously as if he thought he might strike gold. He felt strange, dizzy, as if he didn't know anything anymore. As if everything he had ever learnt as school, at chapel, at home had been sucked out of him suddenly. He couldn't tell Laura about his – Tom Jupe's parents; he couldn't. Just as he knew he had to keep his visits to the South Seas Film Company a secret from his parents, so now he felt desperate to keep the details of his home life from Laura and the rest of the people of the film company. The chapel, the Bible Class, the Temperance Meetings; his father's long hours in the carpenter's shop, making coffins when other work was scarce; his mother's long evenings under the oil lamp with her needle and thread. With a sickening lump in his throat, Tom realised that the reason he didn't want Laura to know all this wasn't just that he was afraid of being found out; no, he actually felt *ashamed* of it all. It all seemed so *dull*, so ordinary, so ridiculous.

'Daniel?'

But what had the parents of Tom Jupe to do with the parents of Daniel Lyons? Surely no more than the Baron of Hatherwick Hall had to do with Laura Merry.

'Daniel!' Laura had stopped her carving and was looking intently at him. 'Is there something *wrong* with your parents then? Are they real ogres?'

A picture flitted across Tom's mind. A picture of a pretty young woman, full of fun. It was a picture he had studied many times. It was in the front of a thinnish booklet, that his mother had bought for Maisie to read. Maisie had read it just once, but Tom – he would have been about eight at the time – had read it over and over again. The booklet told the story of the pretty, young woman – Kitty was her name. She had gone into service in London, but on an evening off, had succumbed to the demon drink, lost her post, got into 'trouble', and ended up living with a one-eyed knife-grinder in somewhere called Hackney.

'I think . . . I think my mother were called Kitty. She went up to a big 'ouse in London as a lady's maid. Then she succumbed to the demon drink.'

'She what?'

'She succumbed to the demon drink.'

From the corner of his eye, Tom saw Laura's jaw drop.

'And then she lost 'er job and got 'erself into trouble –

you know, 'ad a baby.'

'You . . .?'

Tom nodded vigorously, and much encouraged by the rapt attention Laura was giving him, continued:

'She – we . . . went to live with a one-eyed knife-grinder in Hackney.'

Tom paused again, unsure as to how best to get himself from the state of illegitimate knife-grinder's son in Hackney to some other sort of state in the Sussex village of Aduring-by-Sea. Laura looked at him with moist eyes. Tom, remembering how easily the tears came to her, grasped for a happy ending . . .

'But it was all right. In the end. Yes . . . an elderly uncle and aunt found me. And brought me to Aduring. They are very kind. He's a retired sea captain,' he added with a final touch of colour.

Laura was studying her name, which she had just finished carving in the breakwater. 'How old were you then?' she asked, without looking up.

'Can't remember,' shrugged Tom.

'You must have been quite little,' said Laura, 'because you don't speak like someone from Hackney. I know what they speak like in Hackney; I played the Hackney Empire. I was Little Jenny Wren.' Laura paused; but her eyes were still fixed on her carving. 'You speak like someone from down here.'

'I do?' A damp chill raced through Tom's body. He had never thought of himself as speaking any differently from anyone else.

'Oh yes, I was very little, when I came to Aduring. Very little . . .'

A little later, as Laura and Tom began to saunter back along the shore towards the studio, the incoming tide was already washing over the rough etching on the breakwaters – the two names 'Lorrilee' and 'Daniel'.

Chapter Twelve

The posters had appeared overnight on every available spare wall in Aduring. On some large walls, like the side of *The Turk's Head* tavern, which faced an alleyway off Fore Street, there were five or six of them in a line.

'GRAND EVENT!!! THE SOUTH SEAS FILM COMPANY (Prop. Barnaby Merry Esq.) will be giving PUBLIC SHOWINGS OF FILMS!!! (Moving Pictures). Including *Mother's Ruin* featuring the inhabitants of ADURING-BY-SEA!!! and *The Horror at Hatherwick Hall* featuring Mr Bruno Hoogenstadt (formerly Heavyweight Wrestling Champion of the World) and Miss Lorrilee Dupre (Little Jenny Wren). At THE BIJOU CINEMA, South Seas Film Company Studios, Aduring Beach, Saturday 1st August. Performances throughout the afternoon and evening from 2.00 p.m. One Penny. TRULY THE MARVEL OF THE AGE!!!'

Tom first saw the poster when he arrived at school on Monday morning. The phantom advertiser had very astutely pasted a dozen posters in a row along the playground wall. Most of the school had gathered round them and were busily trying to devise ways, be they honest, dubious or downright criminal, of obtaining the princely sum of one penny. It took the presence of Mr Hardacre the schoolmaster in person, and the threat of a 'jolly good thrashing' in particular, to get everyone into school for morning prayers.

As the morning wore on, Tom found himself less and less able to concentrate on Mr Hardacre's arithmetic lesson. Pecks went into bushels, noggins went into pints, pennies went into pounds, but Tom could not have said how much of one went how many times into the other.

His mind was on the poster.

What he really wanted to do was to hide. Of course, he'd known that there was to be a public showing of the South Seas Company's films; Mr Merry had told him so. But still the poster had shocked him. It was as if something special, somewhere secret had been discovered, invaded, ransacked.

It was like . . .

. . . He remembered when he and Ernest had been about eight, they had found a small circle of bushes in the scrub that lay beyond the path on the far side of the river. Inside the circle was a small grassy patch that had become their secret place, their own place, their 'camp' for weeks during the long summer holiday. They had broken off branches from some young trees and had built a roof over the bushes, and had built a trip wire out of a bit of fishing line at the entrance. Then one day, they arrived to find the roof smashed in and the inside patch of grass scorched and blackened by fire. Tom had felt angry, tearful. He had wanted to go and find somewhere else quickly where he could hide.

He felt very much the same now.

He and Ernest had never gone back to their 'camp' in the bushes. And if all of Aduring Village School – or at least as many of them who could manage to get pennies – were to be packed into Mr Merry's boathouse-cinema on Saturday, there was no way he could visit the studio.

He could already imagine the scene; hear the jeers and the catcalls:

'Cor! It's Tom Jupe! Why aren't you at chapel, Tom? 'Ere, it's old Bible-boots! Joop-pee!' He would never be able to face Mr Merry, or Joe, or Laura again.

'Tom Jupe!' Mr Hardacre struck the blackboard with his ruler. His white cane swung on its hook at the front of his huge desk, like a pendulum ticking away the seconds to the hour of execution.

Tom sprang to his feet.

'Yards in a chain, Jupe!'

All eyes faced the front. Everybody knew that the slightest turn of the head would cause the pendulum to stop and the cane to swish and the knuckles to sting.

In the seat next to him, Ernest sat motionless, his hands folded in front of him. Out of the corner of his eye, though, Tom could see his little finger moving to and fro below a number scrawled on his slate.

'Twenty-two . . .? Sir?'

'Speak up, Jupe!' Mr Hardacre was not a man who believed in the concept of doubt and he did not like hesitation and uncertainty in his pupils' answers.

'Twenty-two. Sir.'

'Twenty-two what?'

'Twenty-two yards. Sir. In one chain. Sir.'

'Thank you, Jupe.'

The white cane stayed swinging on the front of Mr Hardacre's desk.

'You owe me one, Tom Jupe,' muttered Ernest in his ear.

Tom stuck to his arithmetic.

Twenty-two yards: one chain. Four pecks: one bushel. Four noggins: one pint.

One village: two worlds.

Chapter Thirteen

'You owe me one, Tom Jupe!'

Although it was Friday, five days after he had saved Tom from the wrath of Mr Hardacre's white cane, Ernest had not forgotten that Tom owed him a favour. Ernest was his father's son. Just as his father always remembered who among his customers was in credit on their account and who in debit – and by exactly how much – so Ernest knew the state of favours between Tom and himself.

'But Ernest . . .'

Tom's protest was understandable, for Ernest had asked him to deliver another two hundred tracts.

'Where they got to be delivered then?'

'Just in the village itself. You already done the far side of the toll bridge and the Beach, ain't you?'

With a guilty pang, Tom thought of the three hundred tracts still sitting, as far as he knew, in a tin box in the boathouse-cum-Bijou Cinema.

'Won't take that long.'

'Why don't you do it yourself?'

'I should've done them after school this week, like, but I didn't and I can't do it tomorrow 'cos I'm in the shop and they gotta to be done by Sunday.'

'Why?'

' 'Cos Valley Road's gotta be done and that's where the Manse is, and if Mr Comfort finds his road hasn't been done, I'll be in for a right ol' ear bendin'.'

Tom's guilty conscience got the better of him.

'If I do it, right, it pays off the one I owe you *and* it gives me one you owe me. All right?'

'All right.'

And so it was that on the afternoon of the first Saturday in August, half of Aduring was staring goggle-eyed at *The Horror at Hatherwick Hall*. Most of the other half was trying, fruitlessly, to squeeze past Mr Barnaby Merry (who stood, chest thrust out, like a ship's figurehead, guarding the boathouse-cinema door) without paying their pennies. But Tom Jupe was gloomily traipsing the streets and alleyways of Aduring, delivering tracts. Determined to make one small act of defiance, he decided, towards the end of the afternoon, to pay a call on Wilf Puttock.

The bell on the door of the barber's shop tinkled merrily.

'Go on through, boy.'

Mr Jessup hovered low over a customer's red neck with his cut throat razor. He grudgingly half raised his head when he saw Tom. He preferred to see customers in his shop, not casual visitors passing through on their way to visit Wilf Puttock out the back. Mr Jessup did have a nice little arrangement with the young photographer though, whereby any male customer who came in to have his photograph taken would be told by Wilf, 'It'd look a lot better if you were just that bit smarter on top, sir,' and the unfortunate customer would be sent through to Mr Jessup for a tuppenny short back and sides.

Tom, for his part, hurried on through the shop, not just because he was keen to see Wilf Puttock, but also because he distrusted Mr Jessup's surly manner and his glittering array of knives and razors.

Wilf Puttock's studio was in fact two rooms: a small cupboard-like dark room and a former conservatory, which gave enough light for Wilf to be able to take photographs without the aid of electricity (of which there was none in the house) or of acetylene lamps (which Wilf couldn't afford).

'Tom Jupe! Thought you'd given me up, boy!'

The young photographer stood in his studio which was set, ready for the next portrait photograph, with a twist-leg table and a large plant. Wilf himself was busy polishing the lens of his brand new Fulmer-Schwig, which was receiving a greater proportion of his attention than was Tom.

'Been busy.' Tom felt awkward, and half-wished he hadn't come.

'So have I, boy! So have I!' Wilf gave Tom a wide wink and Tom's mind flashed back to Whit Monday morning on the riverbank.

Wilf winked at Tom and looked around furtively, as if he was about to impart some great secret. 'And I can tell you something else, Tom, things is looking up.' Wilf spoke in a half-whisper. 'It's like this . . .'

Tom only knew one secret that Wilf Puttock had. His fancy for Maisie. He wondered if he was going to tell him that he and Maisie were secretly engaged. What would his father say? Perhaps Wilf and Maisie were going to elope. Perhaps that was it.

Wilf was still in the middle of his dramatic pause.

'Yes, I knows all about it,' ventured Tom with a broad grin. 'I saw you.'

'Saw me? Saw me what? Down at the Parish Council?'

'Parish Council?'

'That's what I'm sayin', boy. The Parish Council. They gooin' to take me on as Official Parish Photographer!'

'Oh.' Wilf was oblivious to the note of disappointment in Tom's voice.

'It'll be Wilf Puttock who'll be taking photographs at all the big events!'

'What big events?'

'You know – Empire Day Parade and – and that. And I

shall be taking official portraits of the Vicar and Sergeant Grubb! I'm made, boy. I can get a proper studio with shop, like.'

'So you'll be needing a 'prentice even more, now?' Tom wasn't sure why he was saying this.

'Apprentice?' Wilf Puttock looked puzzled. It was obvious that he had forgotten he had ever mentioned the possibility to Tom. 'Did I say to you about it before . . .?'

'Las' time I was in.'

'Oh, yes . . . Well a 'prentice, I should think that's still a possibility.' Tom was sure he had sounded more definite, more enthusiastic the other week, or had he just imagined that, had it just been his wishful thinking?

Wilf's mind was already back on the Fulmer-Schwig. 'Just been over to the Beach and seen them films. You bin?'

'Bin deliverin' tracts.'

'Oh yes.' Wilf yawned noisily, and looked down his tubby nose. 'You didn't miss much, boy, I can tell you. Lot of dancin' about like from those fancy-boy types from London. Make believe and all that. Nothing but a load of jiggery-pokery.'

Tom remembered being in the boathouse-cinema; the pictures flashing over the screen, the tiger, Old Ginger Jenny, the magic, the peals of laughter from Joe and Arthur. Had he imagined it all? Had it been a dream? Were the moving pictures really just a lot of jiggery-pokery? Once at a Bible Class service, he'd had to stand at the pulpit and read a passage from the Old Testament. Without knowing, when he came to turn the page over, he turned two instead of one. The words he was reading were not right, he knew, but they were there on the page. Wilf's words could not be right, but Tom could hear him saying them . . .

'. . . Still if that's the way they earn their living. Now *I* take photographs of *real* people and *real* places. That's what it's all about.'

And Tom knew all he wanted to know.

All the talk about Tom becoming Wilf's apprentice had been nothing more than Wilf's 'big' talk. A few weeks before, Tom would have been devastated by Wilf's seeming lack of commitment to the idea of the apprenticeship, but now he found that it didn't seem to touch him at all. What was the Empire Day Parade, compared with *The Horror at Hatherwick Hall*? What was Sergeant Grubb, still less the Vicar, compared to the gallant Count Peter? Mr Merry, Joe and the rest of them at the Beach *created* people, made new worlds; that was where their magic was. Tom tried to imagine his classmates paying pennies and clamouring to get into Wilf's studios to see his pictures of the Mayor. An impossible scene. He turned to leave.

'I ought to be goin', Wilf.'

'Yeh. Good to see you, boy. Drop by again, eh?'

Tom had just turned the handle of the door leading into Jessup's when a dreadful scream shook the studio. It came from the barber's shop. Tom's pout vanished into a look of terror; but Wilf remained unconcerned.

''S old Jessup. Late Sat'day afternoon's when he gets his pliers out. You get used to it.'

Saturday afternoon, of course. Like many barbers, Mr Jessup ran a flourishing sideline as a dentist.

'I'd hang on a bit like, if I were you, boy. Wait till he's mopped the blood up. It can turn your innards a bit, I can tell you.'

Tom stared at the photographs of various people on the wall. He knew many of them: old Mr Dibble who remembered Queen Victoria's coronation in 1837; Mrs Tanner whose three sons had drowned when their fishing boat had capsized; a large framed sepia tint of Wilf's mother. But the more he stared at the photographs, the more he realised he could see no life in them at all; no hint of mischief, fear or misery.

No sign that their innards might ever turn.

He turned, with a deliberate movement, to Wilf. 'Any message for our Mais then?' He asked it half in anger at Wilf's mocking of Mr Merry's films, half in spite for the cavalier fashion in which Wilf treated his dream of becoming an apprentice photographer.

'What are sayin', boy? What do you know?' Wilf's jaw had dropped a mile.

'Only what I seen with my own eyes.'

Suddenly Wilf seemed to have lost interest in his Fulmer-Schwig. 'You dare go blurting anything out to your father, Tom Jupe!'

Tom played the small boy for all he was worth; and pouting, gave a heavy shrug.

'Here . . .' Wilf dug frantically in his jacket pocket. 'Here's a florin.'

Tom opened the door: blood, teeth, razors, knives – he didn't care. He had to get out. Wilf thrust the florin under Tom's nose.

'What do you take me for, Wilf Puttock? I ain't a kid no more!' With a rough flourish of his hand, Tom knocked the silver coin from Wilf's palm, sending it spinning across the floor.

As he raced through Jessup's shop, now mercifully cleaned of blood splats and broken teeth, Tom heard Wilf's voice still pleading, 'Tom! That apprenticeship, Tom . . .! It's still possible . . .! Tom!'

Chapter Fourteen

Ever since God created the world in six days and took the seventh off, the creatures whom he made in his own image have been inclined to observe Sunday as a day of rest. Not so those of the Primitive Methodist persuasion. Tom's Sundays ran thus: morning prayers, morning service, cold lunch (preceded and followed by an extended grace), Bible Class, tea (preceded and followed by a shorter grace), evening service, then either home or to an aunt's house for hymn-singing; the whole day being nicely rounded off with a Bible reading before bed. The fact that everybody else seemed to have taken a leaf out of God's book and was spending the Sunday resting, made the day's heavy programme even more onerous.

On the Sunday following the 'historical event' of the Beach film show, as Tom, Ernest and his sister Violet walked down East Street on their way to the Chapel (the two boys for Bible Class, Violet to help with small Sunday School children), they passed schoolmates gathering for impromptu games of cricket, younger children bowling wooden hoops and whole families making for the river-bank. Young men and a few daring 'modern' young women weaved and wobbled on sturdy, heavy safety bicycles. The street was full of familiar and half-familiar faces. Ernest, Violet and Tom pushed on against the crowd.

Tom saw her first.

She was in a grown-up, ankle-length dress; pale blue with a high, white collar. With her was her mother, tall and elegant. There was nothing he could do but carry on walking towards them. Ernest was chatting away about a puncture he'd got in his delivery bicycle the day before; Violet walked absent-mindedly just behind them.

The two parties were almost on top of each other before Laura recognised Tom. Her face broke out into a smile of recognition.

'Daniel!'

Tom looked straight ahead. There was a blur of faces in front of him. He collided with a young man pushing a bicycle.

'Oi! Watch it, you daf' young beggar!'

'Sorry!'

'Daniel!' Laura's voice was behind him now, distant.

''Ere, Tom, hang on!' Unconsciously, Tom had begun to quicken his pace and Ernest and Violet were now some way behind.

'Where you haring off to?'

'Don't want to be late.'

'We got plenty of time.'

Tom tried to find a subject of conversation. 'Did you get your puncture mended then?'

'Who was that?'

'Who?'

'That girl!'

'Girl?'

'You saw her, Tom.' Nothing seemed to miss Violet's piercing eyes.

'I seen plenty of girls.'

'You know the one I mean! She smiled at you, Tom Jupe.'

'Never did!'

'Did!'

'Well, I never seen her before.'

'See, you do know the one I mean!' By now, Violet, sensing that she had Tom rattled, was walking alongside him. 'She didn't look your sort, anyway.'

'What do you mean "my sort"?'

'She looked,' Violet paused for effect, actually not totally sure of the exact meaning of the term she was about to employ, 'she looked a trollop.'

'Wash your mouth out, Violet Afflick!' Tom could feel the anger, the injustice of it all rising uncontrollably inside him. Left to her own devices, Violet would have been no match for Tom, but Ernest had to have his say.

'She certainly seemed to know you all right, Tom!'

'How do you make that out?'

'Like Vi said, she smiled at you – and she called out.'

'She called out "Daniel" and my name ain't Daniel and well you know it, Ern!'

'Why did she smile at you then?'

'She must've made a mistake, so stop your stirring, Ernest Afflick.'

'Mistake or not, she certainly did make your cheeks blush, Tom Jupe.'

Further proof, if indeed any were needed, that nothing whatsoever missed Violet's piercing eyes.

Chapter Fifteen

Seeing Laura and her mother in the street had made Tom feel desperately uneasy. The worlds of Daniel Lyons and of Tom Jupe seemed to be lurching inexorably towards each other. Just when he had been looking forward to more excursions onto the Beach, during the school holidays, so the dangers of his being discovered seemed to point to a sudden and painful end to his life as Daniel Lyons.

He had made his way out of the house early again. Judging by the continued black looks Maisie had given him before she left for work, she had already learnt from Wilf that Tom knew of their illicit courtship.

Tom cheerily waved his fishing rod at Amos Carp in the toll gate cottage, hurried over the bridge to the end of the Beach Road and hid his rod in the usual place under the bushes.

He ran along the rough Beach track towards the studio. He had a strange feeling that the great glass studio and the Merrys' wooden bungalow wouldn't be there. That it had all been part of a fanciful dream, like Wilf's offer of an apprenticeship. Part of him almost wished that he had dreamt it all, so that he could go back to being just Tom Jupe. But deeper down he knew the truth: the other world was out there on the Beach, and even if it had been all a dream, there was no going back.

By the time he reached the studio, the skies were already heavy and dark. He made for the boathouse-cinema, hoping he might be able to retrieve the incriminating evidence of his tracts, but Joe was at the door, turning the key in a large, black padlock.

'Dan! H-H-H-ow are you keeping, old chap?' He took Tom's hand and pumped it up and down energetically. Then, he saw Tom's eye on the lock. 'The Guv'nor's g-g-getting jumpy,' he explained. 'He took the news about the London and Britannia fire badly. They lost all their films you know. A whole summer's w-w-work.' Joe sighed. 'They don't really know if the films went up in the blaze, or whether the busters made off with them first – to sell them up North.'

There was a distant roll of thunder.

'The gods are not looking down kindly on us today.' Joe jerked his head towards the black clouds gathered above them. No sooner had he spoken than the first spots of rain hit the boathouse door, spreading out furiously like ink blots in a school copy book. Another clap of thunder seemed to give the tentative drizzle encouragement and very quickly the rain was so heavy it stung Tom's cheeks.

'Come on, Dan! The Guv'nor's got the coffee on.'

They splashed across the shingle to the Merrys' bungalow. Joe hammered on the door and ran straight in.

Even in the stormy gloom, the sitting room still seemed brighter to Tom than his parents' living room did on the sunniest of days. Mr Merry stood with his back to them staring out at the rain as it spat and sprayed off the great glass roof of the studio.

'With a heigh-ho, a heigh nonny no, for the rain it raineth every day,' sang Mr Merry plaintively. He turned and faced Tom. 'So you've taken a fancy to my cawfy, Daniel?'

Tom nodded.

Then Laura came in.

'Hello,' smiled Tom.

Laura's face was impassive. 'Oh you recognise me today, then.'

Tom attempted a look of puzzled innocence.

'Last time you saw me you cut me.' Laura's expression was one of studied disinterest.

'I what?'

'Didn't he, Ma?' Laura appealed to her mother who had just come in.

'I'm sure he didn't. We passed you in the street, Daniel, last when was it –'

'Sunday.'

'Thank you, Laura. Last Sunday afternoon.'

'Oh. Did you?' Tom's cheeks burned like torches. 'I'm sorry.'

'You looked right through me, Daniel.' Laura's eyes were insistent, but quite lacking in concern.

'I don't suppose he saw us, dear. I must say, Daniel, you did look as though you were in another world.'

In another world.

Without a word, Joe handed Mr Merry the key with which he had locked the boathouse door.

'You made sure it was secure, Joe?' Mr Merry was serious.

'It's locked fast, Guv'nor.'

Mr Merry continued to study the falling rain. Then he turned to them all and suddenly said, 'Well, don't just sit there, looking all gloom and doom. What I want to know is, what in the devil's name are we going to do next?'

'Freddie Wells said he'd pop over from Brighton and do his "Mr Dick Takes A Dip" routine,' said Mrs Merry.

'Freddie Wells? He's about as funny as a rainy Saturday in August and just as wet. You know what the people want – they want drama, real drama, not Mr Drippy Dick.'

There was an awkward silence. No one quite seemed to know what to say to Mr Merry in this mood.

Then Laura, stealing a quick look at Tom, curled her legs up under her on the chaise longue and said, 'I have an idea for a drama.'

'Let's hear it then.' Mr Merry's mood still matched the weather.

Laura caught Tom's eye again.

'I don't think I can . . . It's not my story.'

'Then why are you babbling on?' asked Mr Merry tetchily.

Laura unscrambled herself from the chaise longue and went to the door. She beckoned to Tom with a nod of her head. In the hallway she said to him, 'You know what I'm talking about, don't you? Your mother.'

'My mother?' For a moment Tom struggled to make sense of what Laura was saying.

'Yes! Her sad life – and then you being found by your uncle the sea captain and –'

'You think they'll want to make a film of *that*?'

'It's a sad story for you, I know, although it does have a sort of happy ending, but it is a very *real* story, I suppose because it's true. Do you see what I mean?'

'Yes . . . I think so.'

'Do say you'll let Barney make a film of it. He's been so down since he heard the busters had got the London and Britannia.'

'So Joe said.' Tom shrugged. 'Yes, 'course 'e can make a film about . . . about my story.'

Then Laura took Tom's hand and squeezed it. 'Thank you, dear Dan,' she said quietly. 'Barney won't make a mess of it, I know. And we needn't say who it really is about.'

'No.'

Back in the sitting room, Joe and Mr and Mrs Merry all looked up expectantly.

'Dan told me this story, which was why I had to ask him

first.' The only sound in the room was the patter of the rain on the roof. 'There's this girl – from a seaside village like this, very pretty, full of fun. She goes up to London, into service. But she falls in among a bad crowd and ends up with a baby and a husband who's a one-eyed knife-grinder from Hackney. She dies and the boy is left to the mercy of the knife-grinder, but then is discovered by a long lost uncle who's a sea captain and his kindly wife. And they bring him back to the seaside, where he recovers and becomes a new person.

Tom's face blushed redder than the fiercest sunset. His palms felt hot and sweaty. He dared not look up, because he knew that everyone was looking at him.

'That is certainly a touching little tale, my dear.'

'A real ch-ch-ch-oker,' stuttered Joe.

'How did you come by this story, Daniel?' Mrs Merry, the Notting Hill Nightingale, stood magisterially behind the chaise longue.

'It happened to a friend of his,' said Laura quickly.

Mr Barnaby Merry's thoughts were already turning to the practicalities of the project. 'We could get Leonora down to play the aunt . . . Bruno of course would make an excellent one-eyed knife-grinder . . . Laura, the heroine . . .'

She beamed at Tom.

'. . . But who would we get to play the orphan boy though?'

All eyes turned, once more, on Tom.

'Daniel? What a splendid idea! You'll do it, dear boy, of course!'

'But –'

'Oh, the cost? Forget about that. Yes, of course, non-professional actors like yourself usually pay for the privilege of starring in a South Seas Film. But given your interest in the business and the admirable keenness to learn which you have displayed, I'm fully prepared to let you appear in this film without charge. And of course you have provided us with the story, through er . . . your young friend's tragic tale. No, it won't cost you a penny, dear boy. Not one penny!'

Mr Barnaby Merry was himself again.

'W-W-W-When were you thinking of shooting, Guv-'nor?'

'Shall we say next Saturday? Sunlight permitting.'

'Top 'ole! Welcome to the C-C-Company, Dan!'

Like a moving picture itself, the action seemed to be rattling onwards and Tom had no way of stopping it. There was no going back, the drama had to continue to unfold until it reached its climax and its resolution. Excitement and fear surged through Tom's veins. 'I don't know nothing about acting,' he said anxiously to Laura.

'Don't be silly, Dan! It's easy,' Laura grinned, encouragingly.

'But what do you have to *do*?'

'You don't have to *do* anything. You just . . . well, you just have to be yourself.'

Daniel was locked fast in the den and the lions were sitting all around him, purring, smiling.

Chapter Sixteen

At first glance, the gloomy, smoke-filled room above the Public Bar of *The Horn of Plenty* on East London's noisy and bustling Globe Road, might have seemed an unlikely venue for a meeting of the 'trustees' of the Full Gospel Mission to the Kinemagraphic Companies, but anyone with a ladder long enough to be able to peer through its murky windows would have seen at once that the gentlemen gathered therein looked at ease in their dingy surroundings.

There were four 'trustees', all with stern, hard-set faces and shining hair, peering over posters and newspaper cuttings laid out before them on a large mahogany table. Behind them there stood a figure of noticeably different bearing. The cut of his coat, the shine on his shoes, the carefully manicured curves to his fingernails put him in a different class and a different profession altogether. 'I think, gentlemen, you will see why this particular operation deserves your attention.' He spoke in educated, well-modulated tones.

'Yeh. He's not exactly what you could call modest, is he, Mr Jago, sir?' snorted one of the trustees, ' "Truly *The Marvel Of The Age*." ' He was pointing to a poster; a poster more than familiar to the residents of Aduring-by-Sea.

'I've never heard of this Aduring-by-Sea place. Where is it, then?'

'It's a fishing village on the south coast. About eight miles west of Brighton.'

'I've got a sister in Brighton.' This particular piece of information was received with an icy glare from the man they called Mr Jago.

'It is the sort of place where strangers are noticed. It would be prudent, therefore, for just one person to carry out this particular mission.' Jago paused to study his manicured nails. Then he looked long and hard at the only 'trustee' who had not spoken – a tall, wiry, middle-aged man. 'Snook?'

Snook's only response at first was a slight inclination of the head, then the corners of his mouth curled into a weak smile.

'I'll do the job. If it is the Lord's will.'

'Oh it is Mr – or should I say Reverend – Snook, it is.'

There was a low, humourless chuckle from the gathered trustees.

'You have the relevant details, Mr Jago?'

'Indeed.' From a Gladstone bag, the man Jago took a large black-covered book, which had the appearance of a Bible, but was in fact entitled *A Directory of Non-Conformist Chapels in England and Wales Listed by County.* He turned to a page, already marked and read: 'The Primitive Methodist Chapel, Aduring-by-Sea, Sussex. Minister: Reverend G. Comfort, The Manse. Chapel Secretary: Mr Wm. Jupe, 14 Crispin Terrace, Aduring.'

'Come on, Ern!'

'I'm not goin' in them bushes, an' get cut to bits!'

'You're pasty!'

'No I'm not. It's me jacket. If I get it ripped I'll be in for a right thrashing when I get in.'

'It's where we used to have our camp until that Freddie Dibble and the bigger kids smashed it up, don't you remember?'

'Eh . . . Oh yes.' The vaguest memory of summers past

flitted across Ernest's mind. 'What we come here for, Tom?'

In truth, Tom was not sure why he had dragged Ern to the scrub on the far side of the riverbank. It had just seemed a good idea, right somehow, that this should be the place where he would let Ernest into his big secret.

The flat circle of mossy grass in the middle of the clump of bushes bore no sign of ever having been a 'camp', but it was still invitingly quiet and hidden. A few gulls waddled in the muddy reaches of the river, but a distinct chill in the late August air meant that few people were out strolling this particular Friday evening; certainly not – and Tom had found himself looking about to make sure of this – Wilf Puttock and Maisie Jupe.

Both boys chewed on long, milky stalks of grass. Ernest tipped his cap to the back of his head. 'Well?'

And Tom, curiously hunched up with his legs under his chin, told Ernest all about his visits to the Beach and the South Seas Film Company; about Laura, Joe, Mr Merry, the Studio and the film he was to act in – if only Ernest would cover for his absence at Bible Class.

When Tom had finished, Ernest sat for a moment. Then he took off his spectacles, polished them thoroughly and then peered long and hard at Tom, as though he was looking at a total stranger. 'I knew you'd changed.'

'I haven't changed.'

'You gotta stop, Tom. You won't half get a dreadful thrashin' if your dad finds out.'

Tom shrugged, unconvincingly.

'But they're Beach folk, Tom. They aren't our sort!'

'What d'you mean "aren't our sort"?' although Tom knew quite well what Ernest meant.

'They aren't Believers, Tom, and you know it.' Ernest paused, as the gravity of Tom's situation sank in. 'They aren't even Church of England!'

'So?'

'So! Don't *you* believe no more, Tom?' Ernest pleaded desperately with his friend, as he saw his entire world order slipping away beneath him.

'Believe what?'

'Believe . . . believe, you know in the Gospel and that!'

Tom hugged his legs even tighter beneath him. 'There's a lot of things, Ern, that are a proper mystery to me.'

Ernest seemed to be blinking a lot. 'See! They got to you already, Tom. They sown *doubts*!' Doubts no more held a place in the lives or thinking of Primitive Methodists than did drink, playing cards or sins of the flesh.

'I only told you, Ern, 'cos I thought you were my mate! I thought you'd understand.'

'I don't understand nothin' no more.'

The sun was already beginning to set beyond the tree-tops.

'I gotta get back home for supper,' said Tom eventually, but Ernest showed no signs of moving.

'You ain't broken the pledge, Tom?' The pledge all young Prims had signed, along with three million other children and young people, was a promise to 'abstain, with Divine Aid, from all intoxicating Drinks, Tobacco, Snuff and Gambling'.

' 'Course I ain't. I have drunk cawfy though. Twice.'

'This girl we saw Sunday.'

'Laura?'

'She's a real good looker.'

Tom coloured.

'Why she call you Daniel?'

'That's what they think my name is. I mean I couldn't tell 'em my real name, could I?'

'See, it's got you lying.'

'Only 'cos of the chapel and Father. I wouldn't have to go there in secret, if it wasn't for them, would I?'

'Our Vi was that miffed.'

'What about?'

'Your bit of fancy.'

'Don't talk barmy.'

'She's got her eye on you, our Vi has.'

Tom's nightmare picture of his future as a chapel-going carpenter's apprentice came flooding back. 'Come on, we gotta go.' He pushed roughly through the bushes and Ernest followed.

'You will cover for me though, won't you, Ern? This Saturday. You do owe me.'

Ernest sighed. 'Just this Saturday. No more.'

A train from Worthing and the villages beyond hissed and hammered by overhead. The brightly-lit windows stood out like stars and the faces behind them peered down at the reflected light in the river below: Friday night revellers on their way to seek laughter and merriment in the two-penny gallery seats of the Brighton Hippodrome.

The boys ambled towards the ancient wooden toll bridge that led back to the village.

'We are still pals, Ern?'

Still deep in troubled thought, Ernest nodded.

'And you won't tell no one?'

Ernest shook his head. Sensing his friend's uneasy state of mind, Tom sought some sort of reassurance. 'Swear then. You know, the way we did it when we were kids.'

The two boys stood in the middle of the old wooden footbridge over the river, just able to make each other out in the gathering dusk. Ernest crossed his arms over his chest.

'Cross my heart and hope to die; burned and tortured if I lie. There!' He turned and started to run. 'Race you to the end of Fore Street!'

Tom sprinted after him, but although he was soon close

on Ernest's heels, and had plenty of power left in his legs, he made no effort to overtake him.

At Brighton railway station, the Worthing and Aduring train disgorged its excited passengers, who hurried across the station concourse and into the street towards the beckoning lights of the Hippodrome.

The slow train from London arrived at about the same time, and its passengers, too, bustled out of the station like children making for the school playground after a long morning's lessons.

One passenger, though, strolled leisurely down the platform, handing in his ticket at the barrier long after the last merrymaker had passed. His real business in the locality did not start until the next day; he was in no particular hurry. Outside the station, he looked wistfully at the long line of horse drawn and motor cabs, but he carried on walking, with long, loping strides, down Queen's Road towards the town's one Temperance Hotel. After all, riding in a cab would not be thought a fitting mode of transport for a non-conformist minister of religion, particularly one who bore the impressive title of The Reverend Ezekiel P. Snook, Superintendent Minister of the Full Gospel Mission to the Kinemagraphic Companies.

Chapter Seventeen

'Clasp him to your bosom, Leonora!' yelled Mr Merry. Tom found his head propelled into the actress Leonora Lisle's more than ample cleavage. A powerfully-built woman in her late middle years, she was playing the part of the orphan's kindly aunt in 'Daniel's' story. This particular part of the story, where the kindly uncle brings the poor orphan boy back to the seaside from the terror of the one-eyed Hackney knife-grinder, was being shot outside, on the beach. It was a hazy, sultry afternoon, and Mr Merry was trying desperately to hurry the action along, because Joe was afraid that soon there would not be enough light to carry on filming.

'Come on, Dan! Put your arms right round her waist. Grasp her, old son! You're pleased to be here!' Joe waved his arms about excitedly.

Tom was anything but pleased to be there. Reluctantly he threw his arms around the ageing actress's waist. They didn't reach very far.

Mr Merry blew three short blasts on his whistle. 'Go, go, go!' he shouted.

The camera clicked and whirred.

'Relax, luvvy, I won't eat yer,' muttered Leonora Lisle in her thick Cockney drawl.

But Tom couldn't relax. A brooch that Leonora was wearing dug sharply into his chin and the musty scent of her perfume made him feel a little sick. He cursed Daniel Lyons and his silly story. Suddenly he sensed something tickling his nose, then a feeling as if his nostrils were being pinched by a pair of tweezers. He pulled back and found himself peering down into a pair of small, pink eyes. He pulled back further and saw the unmistakable features of the head of a white rat.

With a cry, he broke from Leonora's iron grasp.

'Whoa! Whoa!' roared Mr Merry. 'Daniel, dear boy, what on earth is it?'

'Not 'is fault, Barney! It's my Albert just woke up!' She was stroking the white rat between the ears.

'It's all right, luvvy,' she whispered reassuringly to a goggle-eyed Tom, ' 'e's 'armliss. I got a little pocket for him down me bosom, see, 'e keeps warm that way. I calls him Albert after my first husband. He was a little rat, too.' She let out great peals of laughter. ' 'Ere Bruno, luv!' Bruno Hoogenstadt was behind the camera, waiting for his final scene as the kindly uncle. 'Look after Albert for me, will yer, so he don't get up the boy's nose!'

'Keep away from me wiss that theeng. Else I shall leave ziss feelm ziss second!' blubbered the former Heavyweight Wrestling Champion of the World in alarm, desperately staggering backwards through the shingle: he was terrified of rats.

Laura came over. 'I'll look after him.'

'Just stroke 'im behind the ears, dear, if he gets fretful,' murmured Leonora Lisle.

The 'hugging' scene went off without further hitch. A final shot was taken of Bruno, Tom and Leonora, hand-in-hand, looking out to sea.

The wind had been steadily rising all afternoon, and a salty tang bit into everybody's lips. The white crests of the waves scudded across the surface of the sea, while out towards the horizon, the water looked dark and threatening.

'That's it, everyone,' called Mr Merry.

'Well done, luvvy,' cooed Leonora to Tom, 'you done all right.'

'Hah! Why they want me play good-goody person, hah? Eee-full iss more fun. I like the ee-full!' muttered Bruno, gloomily.

'You can all come back to my place for a tipple,' announced Leonora grandly.

'T-T-T-Top 'ole, Leonora, blinkin' top 'ole,' shouted Joe.

The 'Hackney' part of the film was to be filmed in the studio at a later date. A special set was being built by a couple of carpenters. Indeed Tom had been most surprised, when on entering the studio, he had seen two men in white aprons, hammering and chiselling away just like his father did at Larcombe's workshop. Perhaps the film studio wasn't a different world, after all, but just a parallel one; though whereas the carpenters in the other world hammered and chiselled away at boxes and coffins, the carpenters here hammered and chiselled away at pretend mansions, boudoirs and Hackney slums; and whereas the photographers in the other world took dull portraits of dull village dignitaries, the cameraman here took pictures which told of laughter, misery and joy.

As the adults chuckled and chortled their way back to Leonora's bungalow, Tom found himself alone on the beach with Laura. They stood for a moment watching the bits of flotsam being dragged in by the crashing waves. Tom spotted a bottle amongst the debris. He bent down, picked up a pebble and threw it. It bounced off the neck of the bottle.

'You've gotta hit the bottle,' he explained to Laura.

'Why?'

Tom wasn't sure. ''Cos it's what you do! Didn't they never teach you no games in London?'

'No,' replied Laura, quietly.

'Well, in this game, you gotta hit the bottle.'

Laura picked up a pebble and tossed it at the bottle,

striking it on the neck with a dull ping. 'Easy!' she yelled.

'You're too close,' grumbled Tom.

They both took a couple of steps back. Their pebbles still managed to sing off the bottle with some regularity.

'Where's your ma?' asked Tom.

'In Brighton. She's playing the Hippodrome tonight.' Laura suddenly stopped throwing pebbles at the bottle. 'You didn't mind too much, did you?'

'Mind what?'

'You know, having to live out your past like that. I mean having to think of your poor mother and –'

'I didn't like having to cuddle up to Leonora. I could've been suffocated you know.'

Laura laughed. 'It did look as if she was giving you a bear hug.'

'Huh.'

They made their way back up the beach. The stiff wind and roar of the waves meant that they had to shout to each other.

'I love it when it gets up rough like this!' called Laura.

Tom shook his head. 'It'll mean a storm.'

Laura suddenly stopped and stood quite still. She turned to Tom, then nodded towards the boathouse. A dark figure stood in the shadow of one of the windows, his hand shielding his eyes, peering in. Tom and Laura dropped down onto the shingle out of sight.

'Who's he, Laura?'

'I don't know. I've never seen him before. Come on!'

'Eh?'

'Let's see what he's up to.'

'But – !'

'Come on!'

Tom followed Laura across the shingle, keeping just out of sight of the boathouse. The figure was now walking away from the boathouse towards the road. He had his back to them, but he appeared to be carrying some sort of book.

'Hey!' shouted Laura. 'Hey, you!'

The man turned briefly towards them. Then he began to hurry past the bungalows and down towards the estuary. Laura and Tom staggered up the shingle, but their feet sank deep into the pebbles which kept pulling them back.

'Dan! I'm going to get Barney!' shouted Laura, as they reached the road and she ran off in the direction of Leonora's bungalow.

Tom sprinted across the road, past the Merrys' own bungalow and down over the rough stubble towards the edge of the estuary, just in time to see the figure leap into a small boat and begin rowing furiously for the Dolphin Hard on the far side of the river.

'Come back!' Tom yelled.

He just had time to make out the thin features of his hard-set face.

By the time Laura arrived with Barney, Joe and Bruno, the boat and its occupant were already more than halfway across.

'Damn, damn, damn!' yelled Laura.

It was the first time that Tom had heard a girl swear.

'We could have got him if we'd had a boat!' Laura exclaimed breathlessly to her father, as they sat in Leonora's living room.

'What's your poison, Dan?' asked Leonora, waving a bottle of gin in one hand and a bottle of whisky in the other.

'I expect he's a teetotaller like me, Leonora dear,' said Mr Merry. 'Drink is the curse of the working man,' he added, sounding, Tom thought, uncannily like his own father.

'I wouldn't mind a cup of cawfy, if it ain't too much

trouble,' said Tom.

'Cawfy! The boy demands cawfy! 'E's a proper little performer, ain't 'e! 'E'll be wanting 'is own dressin' room, next.'

There was a burst of loud, good-humoured laughter and both Joe and Bruno slapped Tom on the back.

Only Mr Merry remained silent.

The coffee was duly provided and Mr Merry came and sat by Tom and Laura.

'Do you think he was a buster?' asked Laura. Tom remembered Joe's chilling description of the men paid by some studio owners to destroy other film studios.

Mr Merry shrugged. 'I don't know. But we can't be too careful.'

'Probably some nosy yokel,' said Leonora, without conviction.

'Did you get a decent look at him?' The usual lightness in Mr Merry's voice had disappeared.

'No, I didn't,' said Laura. 'He only turned round once, and his cap was right down over his eyes. He seemed to be carrying some sort of book.'

'Yes,' Tom nodded, 'he was. I saw his face when he got into the boat, an' all.'

'Would you recognise him again?' asked Mr Merry.

Tom sipped his coffee. 'Oh yes, Guv'nor,' he nodded confidently, 'I'd recognise that mean-looking gent anywhere.'

Chapter Eighteen

The motor bus from Worthing shuddered noisily to a halt by the toll bridge. Tom peeped up from his hiding place in the long grass at the side of the Beach road. As the bus clattered away, he saw Ernest walking across the road towards him through a cloud of petrol fumes.

' 'Ere, you would've got this. If you'd been there,' said Ernest sarcastically. 'It's a certificate for delivering the most tracts.' He unfurled a roll of thick glossy paper. 'Presented to Tom Jupe. A True Soldier of Christ!' Ernest read. 'Huh!'

The two boys walked back along Fore Street, and up Hope Street towards their homes in silence. When they reached the Afflicks' butcher's shop, Tom said, 'Thanks for covering for me, Ern.'

'Don't ask me again, Tom.' Ernest's tone was anxious and sad rather than bitter.

The wind was blowing in strong gusts as Tom turned into Crispin Terrace. As he approached number fourteen, he was surprised to see the foggy glow of the oil lamp shining from the parlour window. That could mean only one thing – company.

His mother was in the hall, carrying a tray laden with the best crockery and silver teapot. She nodded in the direction of the front parlour. 'Your father's got a visitor,' she whispered. Then, 'What's that you got in your 'and?'

'Certificate. For delivering them tracts.'

'Is it now? You best go on in, boy.'

Tom opened the parlour door for his mother and followed her into the room. Maisie was sitting in the corner, sewing. She looked up, but the now familiar frosty glare had gone; instead she gave Tom a huge – and it seemed to him, knowing – smile. But hardly had he registered this fact, than his eye was taken by the face of his father's guest.

Even in the dingy glow of the oil lamp, Tom recognised the mean features and stern, hard-set face immediately. As, indeed, he had told Mr Merry he would. For the Jupes' visitor was the man whom Tom had chased over the beach and down to the estuary just a few hours before.

'Ah, this is my boy Tom, Mr Snook,' Mr Jupe was saying. 'Tom, this is Reverend Ezekiel Snook, Superintendent Minister of the Full Gospel Mission to the Kinemagraphic Companies.' Mr Jupe paused. 'In London!' he added enthusiastically.

'Good evening, Tom.' Mr Snook nodded gravely.

'Good evening, sir,' Tom heard himself saying.

'Mr Snook's took a bit of supper with us,' said Mrs Jupe, placing a best china cup and saucer into the minister's long, pale hand.

'Tom's been at a Bible Class convention in Worthing,' explained Mr Jupe. 'Was it a good do, boy?'

Tom nodded, fully expecting that any minute Mr Snook would ask him if he had had a good time on the Beach, but the Superintendent of the Full Gospel Mission to the Kinemagraphic Companies merely continued to sip his tea in silence.

'He's got a certificate for delivering them tracts,' added Mrs Jupe.

Maisie shot Tom another glare.

'We spread the Word as best we can,' said Mr Jupe.

If Mr Snook's smile had been directed at his cup, rather than at Tom, it would have turned the milk in his tea sour.

For his part, Tom stood still as stone, waiting for Mr Snook to condemn him, but the gentleman said nothing.

Perhaps he didn't see me, thought Tom, and instinctively shuffled towards the shadows by the door.

'Mr Snook has felt a calling to conduct a ministry here in Aduring.' There was no disguising the excitement in Mrs Jupe's voice.

The minister carefully put his cup down and placed his hands together in an attitude of prayer. 'Your hospitality, Mrs Jupe, has been very much appreciated.' Mrs Jupe smiled, a little nervously.

'You'd like to be getting back to the Manse?' Mr Jupe was quick to read Mr Snook's thoughts.

'I think so. I would like to rise fresh tomorrow in order to be able to carry out the Lord's work with renewed vigour and dedication.' The minister rose stiffly from Mr Jupe's best armchair. 'Now, I go back up this road, and then, is it second right . . .? Or third . . .?'

'Tom'll go with you, if you aren't sure o' the way,' smiled Mr Jupe, considerately.

The Reverend Ezekiel Snook nodded slightly, picked up a big, black Bible, then turned towards the parlour door, his chilly stare immediately picking out Tom as he lurked in the cover of the shadows.

Chapter Nineteen

'This is really most kind of you, Tom,' said Mr Snook. He bared his teeth in what was no longer a pretence at a bashful smile, but a cold and heartless sneer. Under the yellow haze of the street gaslight, it gave him the countenance of a lean and hungry dog that knows it has cornered its prey.

'Or should I call you *Dan* – the young film actor?'

So Mr Snook had seen him on the Beach. But if he had seen him acting in the film, how long had he been there, watching? Tom recalled with horror the scene that he had played with his head – and Albert the pet rat – buried in Leonora's bosom.

'So our innocent Soldier for Christ is really a lieutenant of the devil?'

'It's nothing to do with the devil!' Tom's words seemed to be lost to the wind almost as soon as they had left his lips.

'Have you bothered to consider your father and mother, boy? What agonies those dear Christian people would suffer if they found that you were nothing more than a poisonous viper cavorting with the devil, putting your soul in danger of the fires of hell?'

Although Mr Snook's long legs made great lolloping strides, and Tom was trotting to keep up with him, it seemed to Tom as if they were making very slow progress indeed towards the Manse, which was only a few short streets away.

'Does anyone else know of the sin in which you are steeped?'

'Only my pal Ern.' Tom's eyes stung with tears and he was sure it wasn't the wind. They walked on in uneasy silence.

'It might,' said Mr Snook eventually, 'it might be a mercy to keep the sordid details of your wickedness from your dear parents. Our God is a merciful one, is he not?'

Tom nodded, in truth doubting even the most basic of beliefs; for at that moment God did not seem to be treating him with any degree of mercy whatsoever.

'Then I will keep the knowledge of your sin within my heart. But you must promise, Tom, never to stray from the path of righteousness in such a way again; never to let yourself be tempted into the company of those kind of people again. For did not Christ Jesus hang from the cross in order that we might be redeemed from our sins in this wicked world?'

The Reverend Ezekiel Snook stopped suddenly, and grabbed Tom's wrist in a fierce grip. His cold eyes peered down into Tom's.

'Let me hear you promise this, Tom. That you will go to the Beach no more.'

A sharp gust of wind whistled around their heads, as if it, too, was keen to witness Tom's vow of obedience. Tom could picture only his parents' faces and he had no doubt in his mind at all when he said, 'I promise.'

'I am glad, Tom. Let this be an end to your deceit. May you grow to be a true soldier for the Lord.'

A sudden sense of relief surged through Tom. He wanted to hug the minister for sparing his parents from the dreadful truth about his sin, and for sparing him from the shame of them knowing. He felt a strange kind of tenderness for the tall, gaunt minister. When they reached the gate to the Manse, Tom said, 'Mr Snook, why did you run off like that?'

'Run off, Tom?' enquired Mr Snook innocently. 'I am

sure I do not understand what you mean. I did leave the Beach in rather a hurry. I was due to be at your parents' house and did not want to abuse their kind hospitality by being late.'

'What were you doing on the Beach then, Mr Snook?'

'Preparing the way of the Lord, Tom.' Mr Snook moved his face even closer to Tom's so that their noses almost touched. Under the gaslight, his cheeks had an eerie, ghostly pallor. Tom could even see the grey stubble on his chin. 'Tomorrow afternoon, Tom, I am to conduct a Mission Service outside the premises of the South Seas Film Company. Your father and Mr Comfort have made arrangements for the congregation and Sunday School and Bible Class scholars of the Aduring Primitive Methodist chapel to be there. You'll be standing there, shoulder to shoulder with me, Tom, helping to call those poor lost souls home to Jesus.'

So that was why he had been on the Beach! Fancy Laura thinking he was a buster! Then the full implication of Mr Snook's pronouncement sank in.

'Outside the Film Company? On the Beach? And I'll 'ave to be there?'

'That's what I said, Tom.'

'But s'posin' . . . s'posin' I'm recognised by someone from the Film Company . . . It'll all come out. That I bin lyin' . . . You will help me, Mr Snook . . .?'

The Reverend Ezekiel Snook, though, was already half-way up the tiny brick path that led to the door of the Manse and either did not hear, or did not choose to hear, Tom's plea.

The strange overwhelming tenderness that Tom had felt for the minister had frozen into fear.

Chapter Twenty

𝕴 t didn't quite rhyme, of course, but that didn't spoil the delight which the half dozen or so small boys obviously took in chanting the natty refrain at the slow, black column of Primitive Methodists as they marched along Fore Street on their way to the toll bridge and the Beach.

The procession was led by the Reverend Ezekiel Snook, with the Prim's own Minister, the Reverend Gilbert Comfort, trotting along in his wake. Tom had manoeuvred himself into the centre of the throng, hoping againt hope that it would prove an inconspicuous place. On one side of him marched Ernest and on the other side Vi, while Maisie and her friend Letty were just behind them. Maisie was still regarding Tom with an air of benign superiority – was it possible that she had learnt something about his visits to the Beach, too? Certainly, the wariness with which she had treated her brother since he had found out about her and Wilf Puttock seemed to have vanished as quickly as it had appeared.

The route over the toll bridge and along the Beach road, once so full of excitement and expectation for Tom, now spelt fear and dread. Tom wondered when the moment of truth would come and who would betray him. Would Laura march up to him and hiss in his ear, 'You cut me again, Daniel!' Would Joe innocently slap him on the back and say, 'H-H-H-How do, old chap?'; or would Vi recognise Laura and simply put two and two together?

The sky was overcast and the breeze still stiff, conditions unlikely to permit any filming, thought Tom with some relief. In fact, the Beach itself was quiet, though as they passed the converted railway carriages and wooden bungalows, he spotted a number of familiar faces peering out at the ragged procession.

As the long solemn line rounded the bend in the Beach road a sudden break in the cloud allowed the sun to burst for a few seconds onto the roof of the great glass studio and there was an audible gasp from the body of the marchers. Mr Snook, however, remained impassive and although the adults quickly recovered their composure, the younger members of the congregation were still enthralled by the shimmering building.

'Ma, it's a fairy palace!' piped up one small voice in awe.

'Nonsense! It's nurthin' but an ol' tomato hot-house turned into the very home of the devil himself!' corrected its parent, waspishly.

The marchers shuffled like an army of black beetles in a semi-circle around the front door of the film studio. The minister stood at their head and raising his hands, muttered a few words of earnest prayer before launching into the first hymn.

'Washed in the blood of the Lamb . . .!'

It was the singing that brought the Beach folk scurrying to their bungalow doors. Among Primitive Methodists, musicality was not a consideration in hymn-singing; the only virtue was loudness.

'Washed in the blood of the Lamb . . .!'

Tom caught a glance at Ernest out of the corner of his eye. Ernest's head was right back and his mouth wide open; with his bulging eyes he looked like a baby sparrow waiting for a feed. Vi was singing lustily too, for this was a favourite hymn of the Afflicks. Tom thought it was probably because of the family business; they felt some sort of special affinity with the words.

'Washed in the blood of the La-a-a-mb!' The final chorus ended with a flourishing roar.

'Oi! Shut that bloomin' racket! Some of us is trying' to kip!' Tom recognised the raunchy Cockney tones of Leonora Lisle somewhere behind him. A few undisciplined members of the congregation turned round, but the majority, only too familiar with the sobering story of Lot's wife (who had been turned into a pillar of salt when she had glanced back to get a last glimpse of the glories of Sodom), kept their eyes firmly on the Reverend Ezekiel Snook as he cleared his throat to begin the sermon.

'Come ye out from among them, and be ye separate!' urged the minister. His long white finger seemed to be pointing directly at Tom. Tom threw his eyes to the right and instantly met the startled glare of Barnaby Merry. Joe and Laura were standing next to him.

Suddenly Tom felt himself letting out a stifled yell as he was pinched violently in the back of the arm. He turned round to face a fiery-eyed Vi. She had obviously recognised Laura.

'Just you wait, Tom Jupe!' she hissed between clenched teeth.

'Woe unto them that call evil good, and good evil!' roared the Reverend Ezekiel Snook, shaking his fist in the general direction of the bemused Joe.

'Amen!' roared back the congregation, their eyes lit up in excited fervour.

Tom turned just in time to see Laura running back towards the bungalow. Then Joe waved to him, a big grin spread across his face. Mr Merry was not so happy, but stood there shaking his head. They turned away and with Joe bidding a cheery, 'Top 'ole everyone!' wandered back to the bungalow, too.

Another text, another hymn, another prayer, another 'Amen!' Then Mr Comfort rose. 'Brethren,' he instructed, 'let us give all we can, for the Lord's continued work among the Kinemagraphic Companies.'

As another hymn was sung, Mr Jupe passed among the congregation, holding out a large carved wooden plate, a plate which he had made himself at Larcombe's workshop. By the time Tom placed his solitary penny on it, the wooden plate was heavy with coins. Tom had never seen so much money in a chapel collection before. But then Mr Snook had spoken with passion and urgency, utterly convincing every God-fearing chapel-goer present of everything that they already believed.

The Reverend Ezekiel Snook raised his hands to the heavens and blessed the offerings that were piled up on Mr Jupe's humble wooden plate. For the Full Gospel Mission to the Kineemagraphic Companies, it had been a good afternoon's work. For Tom, the proceedings had brought only dismay and confusion. Half of him wanted to go and try to find Laura, to try and explain things; the other half told him he wouldn't get anywhere, that he had best forget everything and everybody associated with the Beach. After all, he had promised Mr Snook that he would never talk to 'those kind of people' ever again.

As the Mission Service broke up, Tom stood staring up at the studio, now dull and silvery grey in the afternoon sky.

'What you doing of, Tom Jupe? Waiting for your strumpet?' Vi had made a valiant effort at extending her vocabulary of abusive terms for girls she did not like.

'Be off with you, Violet!' Her sudden appearance had made Tom jump, and this as much as anything else had made him angry at Violet's taunting.

'You just wait. I'm goin' to tell about you and . . . and 'er!'

'Tell what?'

'That you made eyes at 'er.'

'Rather make eyes at 'er, than make eyes at you, Violet Afflick.'

'And that you ain't a proper Christian!'

'You don't know nothing.'

'No? But I bet Ern does!'

And with that very acute observation, Violet stomped off.

Tom walked home at the back of the gathering. He did not dare look up at any of the bungalow windows as he meandered down the Beach road; he was too ashamed, too angry. He had never felt so wretched in his whole life. Perhaps this was all God's punishment, to pay him out for all the lying.

Out in front, the Reverend Ezekiel Snook was deep in conversation with members of the congregation, both old and young. If he had been a music hall artiste, you might have described him as Top-of-the-Bill; if he had been a film actor, he would have been a star.

'You all right, Tom?'

With a start Tom realised that his mother had held back from the enthusiastic throng to wait for him.

Tom nodded thoughtfully.

'What do you make of our Reverend Ezekiel Snook, then?' There was an unexpected touch of sarcasm in her voice.

Tom said, 'I never seen more money in the plate.'

'Yes,' said Mrs Jupe between tight lips, 'your father's very pleased.'

'You don't like him, do you, Ma?'

'Judge not, that ye be not judged, Tom. But . . . oh, I don't know . . . so he comes from London? Now, do it say in the Good Book that London is any nearer to heaven than Aduring?' She sighed. 'There's somethin' about his *manner*, Tom. I expect it's a London manner, Tom, and I'm jest not used to a London manner.'

So his mother felt uneasy about Mr Snook, too! Tom dearly wanted to tell her that Snook had threatened him, but that would have meant telling her about the Beach and the films and Laura and acting . . . everything. So instead, he said, 'Ma, if you want someone to do something like, is it a Christian thing to threaten to do summat nasty to 'em to make 'em do it?'

'No, I wouldn't have thought so.'

'S'posin' the thing they want you to do – s'posin' they *make* you promise you'll do it.'

'No one can make you promise nothin', Tom. Mark my words. A promise is a promise only if it comes from the heart.'

Chapter Twenty-one

A special tea in the Sunday Schoolroom – the Reverend Ezekiel Snook said the grace. Evening service in the chapel – the Reverend Ezekiel Snook read a lesson. Hymn-singing at the Manse – the Reverend Ezekiel Snook sang a solo. Tom was relieved to be able to crawl into bed in his tiny attic room, just to get away from the man.

Only he found he couldn't.

Over and over in his mind whirled the images of the last two days. The Reverend Ezekiel Snook on the Beach, running away; the Reverend Ezekiel Snook's sneer as he had threatened him under the gaslight; the Reverend Ezekiel Snook's eyes when he saw the pile of brass and silver on the wooden collection plate.

His promise to Snook had come from nowhere near his heart, he knew that. He had to go and try and explain to the Merrys that he was really Tom Jupe.

And there was the rub.

For it was obvious to Tom that to go and explain to the Merrys that he was really Tom Jupe would mean having to get rid of Daniel Lyons, once and for all. Tom thought back to his first visit to the Beach – watching the film of the Temperance Service fracas with Ginger Jenny . . . how Mr Merry had laughed about Bible-bashers . . . telling Tom that the London and Britannia had actually had a group preaching outside their studios –

The London and Britannia! The studio that had been destroyed by busters! It was suddenly more than obvious to Tom, that Snook was no more the 'Reverend' Ezekial

Snook than he was . . . well, than he was Daniel Lyons.

Tom threw back the sheets. He dressed quietly, and carrying his boots, made his way to the steep cottage stairs. He slid down the banister, side-saddle fashion. Not until he was through the back yard and into the twitten, did he dare put on his hob-nailed boots.

As so often happened on the coast, the wind, which during the day had died down, was, with the coming of nightfall, beginning to gust again. The storm that had threatened over the last two days, now seemed likely to break at any moment.

Tom ran out of the twitten and on down East Street to the Dolphin Hard. The pubs along Fore Street were still busy, bright and noisy, but the night itself was as dark as the soul of the devil himself. Tom slipped down the Hard to the water's edge. This time, under cover of darkness, he would make the trip to the Beach the quick way, across the estuary, rather than walking all the way along Fore Street and out over the toll bridge. Rowing-boats and dinghies lay scattered just above the high-water mark. Tom crawled between them, until he spotted the one he was looking for. It was smaller than the rest and belonged to Wilf Puttock. Tom put his shoulder behind the bow and the boat slid gently through the mud, and into the dark waters of the river estuary.

The rising wind was making the water choppy and Tom could feel it pulling at the boat and sense the pushing of the current beneath the keel. He pulled hard on the oars, knowing that any slacking in his rhythm would lead to the boat – and him – being swept downstream towards the harbour mouth and the open sea. He leaned forward, pulled back; leaned forward, pulled back; all the time keeping an eye on the slowly fading lights in the backs of the Fore Street pubs. He glanced over his shoulder, but it was too dark to see any lights on the Beach. He leaned forward, pulled back; leaned forward, pulled back. He had rowed a dinghy many times; with his father, with his cousins, with Ernest; but never before alone, never before in the dark, never before against such a wind, never before into the unknown.

Strange, dark shadows seemed to play on the surface of the water. Then with a sense of relief, Tom realised that they were the weeds and grasses which grew along the water's edge on the Beach's river shore. He felt the keel scrape the bottom of the river and pulling hard on the oars, he ran the boat up onto the shore.

He pulled the boat clear of the rising tide and looked about him to try and establish whereabouts on the Beach he had landed. He could see nothing. He picked his way carefully up the Beach until he could make out the shape of a bungalow. It was Leonora Lisle's, just two along from the Merrys'.

As he approached the Merrys' bungalow, he could just make out the dim light of oil lamps shining behind the curtains. They were obviously still up.

'Hah!'

Suddenly, Tom's neck was jerked from its socket in a vice-like grip.

Leggo! Tom wanted to cry, but found he could only manage a gasp and a gurgle. He thrashed about wildly with his arms, but the harder he hit out, the tighter the armlock around his neck became. He saw lights flashing before his eyes. They got closer and closer before he realised they were lamps.

Through the yellow glow of the lamps, there flickered the familiar faces of Barnaby Merry and Joe.

'Iss the boy! Iss the boy!' cried an excited voice on the end of the armlock: Bruno Hoogenstadt, former Heavyweight Wrestling Champion of the World.

In the bungalow, Bruno sat Tom down in one of the

wicker chairs. Laura came in, wearing a dress and pinafore, followed by her mother who was wrapped in a long, pale dressing gown. Everybody looked down accusingly at Tom: Laura, her mother, Mr Merry, Joe, Bruno – even the pictures of actors and music hall artistes seemed to stare down at him from their frames in contempt.

'Are you going to give us a sermon or sing us a hymn?' asked Laura, coldly.

'Laura! That's enough!' Mr Merry spoke with an anger and authority that Tom hadn't heard before. He turned to Tom. 'Let's hear what you've got to say for yourself, Daniel Lyons.'

'Well, y'know when Laura and me saw that man snoopin' round yesterday and I said I'd recognise him any-where, well I have and he's the Reverend Ezekiel Snook.'

'He's the who?'

'Ezekiel Snook, Superintendent of the Full Gospel Mission to the Kinemagraphic Companies. The preacher you saw this afternoon and 'e grabbed me last night and I had to promise him I'd never come 'ere again like and that I wouldn't split on him else he said he'd tell my dad I been comin' 'ere and that'd be real trouble.'

'Your dad being a one-eyed knife-grinder from Hackney?'

Tom gulped and said quietly, 'My dad being a two-eyed carpenter from Aduring. We're Prim see.'

'Y-Y-You certainly are, Dan!' mused Joe.

'And that's another thing. My name ain't Daniel Lyons. It's Tom Jupe. But I couldn't tell Laura that, could I, in case it got back and I wanted to keep coming here because it's the best place in the world and . . . and . . .' He trailed off, lost in a desperate rush to get his own story out. Why had it been so much easier telling Laura about the 'life' of 'Daniel Lyons'?

Mr Merry shook his head slowly. 'The boy's been in half

a film and he's already got himself a pseudonym!' And he burst into a great chuckling smile, which slowly was picked up by Laura, her mother, Joe and even Bruno.

'But Guv'nor . . .'

'Say no more, Tom!'

'But –'

'Let's have a cup of cawfy and toast the visit of our new friend, Tom Jupe, here. I'm sorry my boys set about you, like that, young Tom, only we've all been a bit jumpy round here of late –'

'But Guv'nor!' Tom found himself almost screaming. 'I come to warn you, I think Snook's a buster!'

Suddenly, the whole room seemed to shine with a warm, clear light. Tom turned towards Laura. The light seemed to be getting brighter.

'Oh my God, Barney!' Mrs Merry shrieked. She was pointing towards the window.

The lightest, brightest place of all.

'It's outside, Guv'nor! It's the studio!' Joe, Bruno and Mrs Merry raced to the door, followed by Laura and Tom.

On the other side of the Beach road, the whole of the inside of the studio seemed to be alight. The great glass building glowed red and orange against the black and stormy sea.

'The pump!' yelled Mr Merry. He, Joe and Bruno raced off to the water pump, although even now it seemed too late to save the studio. The whole area was lit with a strange grey light. A movement on the other side of the bungalow suddenly caught Tom's eye. A tall, loping figure –

Laura! It's him!'

Tom raced round the back of the bungalow towards the swiftly striding shadow of the Reverend Ezekiel Snook.

'Laura! Come back!' called Mrs Merry, but Laura was only a couple of paces behind Tom.

'He's got a boat again!' cried Laura despairingly.

'So what,' yelled back Tom, 'this time so've I!'

Chapter Twenty-two

'Keep your eye on that light!'

'Why?'

'It's the back room at *The Dolphin*, that's why. We gotta head for it.'

If anything the wind and current were even stronger now than when Tom had rowed over to the Beach. Behind him, Tom could see the flames from the studio fire lighting up the Beach. There was a rumble and a crash, and a shaft of silver lightning streaked down the length of the sky. The rain began to fall heavily in great slanted sheets.

'I saw him! I saw him in the lightning!' yelled Laura excitedly. 'He was running up a kind of little slope by the building where the light is.'

'That's the Dolphin Hard. That's where we're heading.'

Lean forward, pull back; lean forward, pull back.

Another flash of lightning and Laura was saying, 'I can see it! We're almost there, Dan!'

Tom felt the keel of the boat scrape on the riverbed. To save time he leapt out of the boat, rocking it dangerously, and knee deep in water pushed it the last few metres up onto the hard. Laura scrambled out after him.

'Which way?'

'I 'spect 'e's gone down the Manse. That's where 'e's stayin'. Come on!'

The now torrential rain had turned the dusty streets of Aduring into a sloshy, smelly quagmire of mud and horse dung. Tom and Laura ran on past *The Tiger's Head* and up Hope Street, their clothes clinging to their bodies with the wet and their hair hanging in dripping rats' tails about their ears.

'There he goes!'

Snook disappeared round the bend by St. Cosmo's Church.

'He's got the film box with him, Dan!'

'The what?'

'The metal box Barney keeps all the films in! He's got it under his arm. He's stolen all our films!'

'If we cut through the churchyard and up the twitten, we come out at the Manse and we can cut him off!' yelled Tom triumphantly.

On they ran, past grey gravestones, glinting in the wet moonlight; then up the narrow alleyway, Laura close on Tom's heels. But when they came out at the Manse, there was no sign of Snook anywhere.

'He can't 'ave beaten us to it! He must've gone somewhere else!'

'Where? Where would he go to?' asked Laura desperately.

A piercing whistle from an approaching train split the air.

'Blimey!I got it!' And Tom was off again. Back down the road into Hope Street and northwards, Laura chasing after him just a few paces behind.

The crossing gates were down. The London train clattered through, then clanged and hissed to a halt at the station platform. Tom stumbled up the steps of the footbridge. Laura grabbed the handrail for support as she tumbled after Tom down the other side.

'Stop! Stop!' cried Tom, leaping off the last four footbridge steps and onto the station platform. But his lungs were exhausted and his voice was weak. His words were merely carried into the deafening hissing and puffing of the great mustard-coloured engine.

'Aduring-by-Sea! Aduring-by-Sea! Adur*ing*!' John Jarrett Esquire stationmaster stood with his legs astride, intoning the familiar chorus, which too, was hardly heard above the engine.

The stationmaster bade good evening to the tall, gaunt gentleman travelling first class and closed the carriage door for him. Then he blew his whistle, waved his lamps and –

'Oi!'

– was rudely pushed aside by a drowned rat of a boy, who grabbed the handle of the carriage door and pulled. As the engine panted, then roared and gathered speed, the door flew open.

A flash of metal and the boy fell senseless to the ground, a red streak across his forehead showing where he had made contact with the metal box that had been swung at him by the only occupant of the compartment.

'Dan! Dan!' A mud-stained, bedraggled girl dropped to her knees beside her companion.

The stationmaster lumbered up and took one quick look at the prostrate figure of the boy. 'Dan? That's Jupe's boy, that is, young Tom Jupe.'

'I *know*!' sobbed the girl frantically, 'I know who he is! Do something! *Please*!'

'Fred!' yelled the stationmaster across the tracks to the lumbering youth who was his assistant porter. 'Over 'ere! And make it snappy!'

And so it was, some ten minutes later, that Mr Jupe opened the front door of 14 Crispin Terrace to find John Jarrett Esquire stationmaster and Fred Dibble his assistant porter standing, wet and shining, at either end of a porter's trolley. On the trolley were laid half a dozen or so Post Office sacks; under the sacks was the unconscious figure of

Mr Jupe's one and only son.

'Oh my dear Lord, what has bin 'appenin'?' Mr Jupe bent down over Tom.

'Let's get 'im in out of the weather, fust, Will.'

Windows and doors were opening all round them.

'Everythin' all right, Will?'

'Tom's 'ad a bit of an accident, that's all.'

The word went up the street: 'Jupe's boy. 'Ad an accident.'

'Is 'e bad?'

'Dunno. See whether they send for the doctor or the undertaker.'

Mr Jupe and the stationmaster carried Tom through the narrow doorway of the cottage and into the hall, where Mrs Jupe stood shaking and trembling in her nightgown.

'Get you back to the station, Fred Dibble!' yelled the stationmaster, as his young assistant porter shuffled about on the doorstep, gawping at Maisie Jupe in her nightgown and hair hanging loose down her back.

'I took the liberty of calling Doctor 'Erriot on the station telephone,' explained the stationmaster. 'He's on 'is way.'

'Oh for goodness' sake get him up to bed and get those filthy wet clothes off of him, I can't have Doctor 'Erriot seeing him like that!' sniffed a distraught Mrs Jupe.

'Then show us some light with that blessed candle, woman!' snapped Mr Jupe.

They laid Tom out on his bed in the attic room. Mrs Jupe and Maisie made him presentable for the doctor, much as they might dress the goose for Christmas dinner.

'What's this all about, John?' asked Mr Jupe, quietly.

'Better ask the girl, she 'er chasin' 'im.'

'What girl?'

The stationmaster turned round but there was no sign of Laura. At that very moment, she was stumbling over the toll bridge towards the Beach road.

'Perty yun thin' she were, an' all . . . I sin 'er about the village o' late . . .'

Tom groaned and opened his eyes.

''E's come round, Ma!' cried Maisie.

'Oh my boy! Tom! It's all right, Tom, you're back home now.

Tom closed his eyes.

''E's jest 'ad a nusty bump, that's all,' said the station-master philosophically, 'but he'll prob'ly 'ave a 'ead like a smithy's anvil in the mornin'.'

Tom opened his eyes again.

'Mary! Oh there y'are. Is the boy all right? What on earth happened to him?' Tom's Aunt Edie from three doors down.

Tom closed his eyes again.

'We don't know.' Mrs Jupe shook her head sadly.

'I dunno 'ow 'e came to be at the station, but I can tell y'how he got that there bump,' said the stationmaster with an air of some self-importance. ''E were 'it, Will. By a metal case a-wielded by a railway passenger.'

He paused and shook his head uncomprehendingly. 'And a Fust Class passenger, at that!'

'Did you know this 'ere passenger?' asked Mr Jupe, impatiently.

'I wouldn't say 'as 'ow I *knows* 'im,' pondered the sta-tionmaster. His mind, like his trains, ran like clockwork and he was never to be hurried. 'But I knows *of* 'im. 'E arrived yes'day mornin' on the nine fifteen from Brighton and asked 'is way to the Manse.'

'You can't mean the Reverend Ezekiel Snook?' gasped Mr Jupe.

John Jarrett Esquire shrugged. 'Like I said, I don't *knows* 'im, only knows *of* 'im.'

'Tall, mean-lookin' . . .?' suggested Mrs Jupe.

'That's the fella! Evil-eyed old varmint, begging your pardon,' confirmed John Jarrett. 'Your boy were struck down by one of your own and a Reverend one at that.'

'What's it all *mean*, Will?' asked Mrs Jupe despairingly.

'I rang through to Hove, they'll pick 'im up there,' John Jarrett assured her.

There came the sound of a trap arriving outside. 'Mr Jupe!' called a rich, Scots voice. Doctor Herriot had arrived. The inhabitants of Crispin Terrace duly registered the fact that it was the doctor's and not the undertaker's trap and so one by one closed their doors and windows on that night's excitement.

Chapter Twenty-three

Tom opened his eyes and the hammering burst out all over his head. The sun was streaming in from the window behind him, directly onto Maisie who was sitting by the side of his bed.

'Mais?'

'Lummy, Tom, you've 'ad us frittened out of our wits.'

'My 'ead 'urts.'

'I ain't surprised.'

Tom half closed his eyes against the light. 'Does they know?'

'Does they know what, may I ask?'

Tom didn't know where to start; if to start.

Maisie said, 'They knows you were walloped one by that old goat Snook.'

'Oh.'

Maisie paused and winked at her young brother. 'But they dunno about your girlfriend.'

Tom sat bolt upright. 'I ain't got no girlfriend!' His head sang and screamed.

'Lie down, boy, and shut up, afore you wake Ma.'

Tom flopped down onto his pillows.

'Vi Afflick told me you'd bin makin' eyes at a girl on the Beach. She reckoned you bin seein' her. Said she were a trollop. I guess that means she's pretty. And I guess it were the same girl Old Jarrett was on about.'

Tom groaned and wished he hadn't woken up.

'I seen you comin' back from along the Beach road, and hidin' in the grass, anyhow.'

'When?'

'Saturday evenin –'

'You never said nurthin' to Dad or Ma?'

'No, why should I?' asked Maisie, innocently.

Tom knew his sister was all right really, but he also knew she wasn't *that* all right. 'Jest in case I decided to get my own back,' he said, quietly.

'What do you mean?'

'Jest in case I decided to say summat about you and that Wilf Puttock, that's what I mean.'

Maisie narrowed her eyes at her brother. 'Yes, how *did* you find out? I thought we were that careful.'

'Saw you spooning up by the river.'

Maisie blushed like a rose. 'You never did!'

Tom nodded. 'I reckon we better call it evens.'

'Yeh . . . Evens.'

There was a pause while Maisie seemed to study her brother in a fresh light. 'Who is she, then, Tom?'

' 'Er dad owns the Film Company, but she calls him Barney. She does acting. Her real name's Laura, but her acting name's Lorrilee Dupre.'

'Is she to do with Adelaide Dupre, then? She's lovely . . .'

'That's her ma. Only her real name's Elsie.' Tom suddenly caught up. ' 'Ere! How do you know about all that? You ain't been goin' to the Variety, 'ave you?'

Maisie lowered her voice to a barely audible whisper. 'Wilf took me, over at Brighton.'

'Does Dad know?'

'Has the bump on your head affected your brain?'

'Does Ma know?'

Maisie looked thoughtful for a moment. 'I reckon she might, you know.'

Tom said, 'You don't think films are bad then?'

'Bad? Some of 'em are bloomin' terrible!'

'You know what I mean, Mais.'

'Why should I?' Maisie was at the window, staring down into the street below. 'One of these days, I'm going to get married and leave home. And then it won't matter what Dad and Ma think, it'll be up to me to decide what I think is good for me, or bad for me.' She turned back towards Tom. 'And the same'll be happenin' to you one day. You ain't goin' to be "the Jupes' boy" forever.'

'You'd like me to be workin' for Wilf, eh, Mais?'

Maisie grinned. 'Might be handy.'

Tom gave a long sigh. 'I reckon we better call it fains for good, Mais.'

Maisie nodded. 'Yes, it's about time, boy. It's about time.'

After Maisie left for work, it became a morning of drifting. Tom drifted in and out of a light sleep, the sun drifted in through the open window and across the bed; his mother and various neighbours drifted in and out of the room.

Just before his father had gone to work, he had heard him and his mother whispering loudly on the landing outside.

'. . . We got to find out sometime, Mary.'

'Let 'im get over it fust, Will, for goodness' sake . . .'

In both his waking and his half-sleeping moments, Tom's head seemed to be filled with questions he knew he would eventually be asked.

So many questions. So many answers.

About mid-morning, he heard Ernest's voice downstairs, but when Mrs Jupe showed him up, Tom appeared to be fast asleep.

Lunchtime. It must be. Tom could just make out his father's voice downstairs, and another voice which it took him but a moment to recognise. Footsteps on the stairs. The voices getting clearer.

The bedroom door opened.

'Ah boy, so you're awake then! Brought a vis'ter to see you.'

Behind his father, a familiar girth filled the doorway. 'Tom, dear boy! How are you feeling?' asked Mr Barnaby Merry.

Chapter Twenty-four

om looked from his father to Mr Merry and back again. Each had half an eye on Tom and an eye and a half on the other man. Now that these representatives of both his worlds were together in one room, Tom felt not a little scared.

Mr Merry went to one side of his bed and his father to the other.

'You got some explaining to do, my boy,' said Tom's father severely.

Tom heard the shouting and laughter of children playing tag in the street and wished above all else that he could be an innocent eight-year-old once more, unaware of the world beyond chapel and home.

'Well?' Tom's father demanded.

But before Tom could draw breath to answer, Mr Merry had butted in. 'We first met Tom, when he came delivering these!' He waved a familiar looking leaflet in his hand: '𝕽𝖊𝖘𝖎𝖘𝖙 𝖄𝖊 𝖙𝖍𝖊 𝕯𝖊𝖛𝖎𝖑, 𝖆𝖓𝖉 𝕳𝖊 𝖜𝖎𝖑𝖑 𝕱𝖑𝖊𝖊 𝖋𝖗𝖔𝖒 𝖄𝖔𝖚!!!' it screamed.

Tom's mind was a whirl as he realised that Mr Merry must have found the tracts he had dropped in the boat-house!

'I knew I should never've let him go in the fust place,' muttered Mr Jupe, warmly.

'The boy came to no harm while he was with us!' Mr Merry met Mr Jupe's steady gaze. Tom could feel the tension between the two men and he feared the worst.

'I will not have voices raised in anger in this house!' The

command came from Tom's mother, standing in the doorway, arms across her chest.

Both Mr Jupe and Mr Merry shrank back a little.

'I think,' Tom's mother continued, 'we could all do with taking stock. For a start, you'd do well to remember the japes you got up to when you were a thirteen-year-old lad, Will Jupe, before you start beholding the mote in your son's eye.' Mr Jupe shuffled uneasily. 'And as for you, Tom, pretending to us that you were at the Bible Class Convention – when you were elsewhere, that was an act of deceit and you'd do well to think about it.' Tom wriggled uncomfortably in his bed. 'And as for you, Mr Merry, I do not propose to cast judgement upon the morality of making moving pictures, but running amok into innocent worshippers in the village street was an act unworthy of even the commonest street urchin.'

'Indeed, ma'am.' Mr Merry looked crestfallen.

'Even if, since that day, Old Ginger Jenny's not touched another drop – and she's started coming to chapel regular,' added Mrs Jupe.

'Indeed, ma'am,' said Mr Merry again.

But Mrs Jupe had already left the bedroom and was halfway down the stairs.

Mr Merry struggled to find something to say. 'A fine boy you've got there, Mr Jupe,' he managed at last.

'Well, me and Mrs Jupe 'as tried to bring 'im up proper – and 'is sister.' There was an unmistakable touch of pride in his father's voice.

Tom decided it was time to ask a few questions. 'Did he get away?' he ventured.

'They searched the train for 'im at Hove, but 'e'd 'opped it. Reckon 'e knew what was up and 'opped out of the carriage on the other side, then made 'is way 'cross the sidings and out through the coal yard,' explained his father.

Mr Merry shook his head sadly. 'It was a clever disguise,

acting the character of an evangelist, like that. You see, he could go anywhere, clutching that big black Bible of his, and nobody would have the slightest suspicion.'

'So I was too late,' mumbled Tom. 'He still managed to burn down the studio and get away with the films.'

'And with the biggest collection ever took by the Prim,' added Mr Jupe, bitterly. 'You should be thankful you did-n't get hurt wuss, boy.'

'Oh! The studio was only a *building*, after all,' said Mr Merry airily, 'it can be rebuilt. He didn't get away with the films though, Tom. They're quite safe.'

'But how . . . if he got away? He had the film box with 'im. That's what 'e 'it me with!'

'So he did, the blaggard! But there weren't any films in it. As soon as I got wind that there might be a buster about, I took all the films out of the boathouse and kept them under our bed – where they are at this very moment. No, all Snook got from the boathouse was the metal box.'

'And it was empty, was it?' asked Mr Jupe.

Tom felt his cheeks burning.

'Not exactly *empty*,' said Mr Merry, with a knowing wink at Tom.

The 'Reverend' Ezekiel Snook drew the curtains on what little murky light was penetrating the upstairs room of *The Horn of Plenty* on London's Globe Road and faced the film and cinema entrepreneur Mr Charles Jago across the green baize covered table. It was three days since Snook had fled Aduring-by-Sea, and for two and a half of them he had been on the road, taking a devious route back to London that avoided all obvious main roads and all areas of popu-lation where sharp-eyed constables might be tempted to hail him with awkward questions.

'It's a bad business, Snook,' growled Jago, a thick cigar butt bobbing up and down between his front teeth. 'I expected a professional job. The way you appear to have performed on this last little operation seems to have been little better than a poor music hall turn!'

'Look here, Mr Jago, I wasn't caught; I fired their premises like you said and I've got their films!' He made no mention of having also got away with the largest collection ever taken at a Prim service in Aduring, the bulk of which was nestling in his inside pocket. He dropped the metal film box down on the table with a dull thud. He took a burglar's pick-lock from his pocket and began carefully turning it in the lock that held the lid fast.

There was a quiet click as the lock sprang.

The 'Reverend' Ezekiel Snook turned the box upside down on the bright green baize.

Out of the metal box – the same metal box that had dealt such an ugly blow to the head of Tom Jupe, the same metal box that the 'Reverend' Ezekiel Snook had been gripping tightly under his arm for three days on the road from Aduring-by-Sea – there fell, not the complete works of the South Seas Film Company, but two hundred and ninety-nine religious tracts, bearing in fearsome black letters the timely instruction 𝕽𝖊𝖘𝖎𝖘𝖙 𝖄𝖊 𝖙𝖍𝖊 𝕯𝖊𝖛𝖎𝖑, 𝖆𝖓𝖉 𝕳𝖊 𝖜𝖎𝖑𝖑 𝕱𝖑𝖊𝖊 𝖋𝖗𝖔𝖒 𝖄𝖔𝖚!!!

'Snook! Explain this! Snook! Come back here!'

Ezekiel Snook resisted the furious demands of his master and fled *The Horn of Plenty* as fast as his long legs could carry him, his days as a film 'buster' well and truly over, but the collection from the Prim congregation jangling like a peal of bells in his jacket pocket.

Chapter Twenty-five

Tom spent a further two days in bed and though he would not have cared to admit it to anyone, he rather enjoyed being at home, on his own in the familiar little room he had known as his ever since he could remember. Perhaps what he was really enjoying was being Tom Jupe. And, as Tom Jupe, he'd had a lot to think about.

Once Doctor Herriot had given the word though, Tom, suitably bandaged around his head, made his way along Fore Street and out over the toll bridge to the Beach road.

The once glittering studio was a shell of twisted metal, shattered glass and blackened brick. A few recognisable pieces of the once splendid wooden scenery – Hatherwick Hall, the pauper's kitchen and the ladies' boudoir – stuck out at ugly angles amongst the charred remains.

'D-D-Don't worry about it, old chap, we can build another.' Tom hadn't seen Joe sidle up beside him. 'Go on over to the bungalow. You'll find the Guv'nor there!'

Mr Merry was sitting at his desk, exactly as he had been when Tom had first met him at the beginning of the summer. After enquiring at great length as to the state of Tom's health, and praising in the fullest terms the qualities of Tom's parents, Mr Merry finally paused to draw breath.

'Guv'nor . . .'

'What is it, dear boy?'

'Did you tell Dad about me being in the film and me telling you I was an orphan and –'

'Good gracious me no! None of that was appertaining to the story in question, was it? And anyway, if I recollect, it all concerned one Daniel Lyons, did it not? Obviously, a different boy, entirely.'

'Thank you.'

'Thank *you*, dear boy.'

'I'm sorry about that story I . . . er . . . Daniel made up – about the orphan boy . . .'

'Never mind, perhaps we can finish it next year, sunlight permitting.'

'No, I mean about me having made it up, about it not being true.'

'Not true? Of course it's true! Oh it may not have actually *happened* – to you or to anybody else – but it's still true.'

Tom frowned at him, lost for a moment in the search to make sense of what Mr Merry was saying.

'It's like this – our hero is unloved and his step-father, the –'

'– One-eyed knife-grinder from Hackney –'

'That's the fellow. He's cruel to the boy and the boy is dreadfully unhappy. But enter stage left the old sea captain and his sister; they are kind to the boy and we all end up going away happy. Yes? So the truth, and all right it may be a very corny and simple one but it's none the worse for all that, is that it's better to be kind and loving to our fellow beings than cruel to 'em.'

Tom stared thoughtfully through the window to the space where the studio used to be.

'If you're looking for Laura, dear boy, she's down on the Beach.'

Tom found her sitting by the breakwater, where a few weeks before they had carved their names in the slimy wood. She was throwing pebbles at an old bottle that had been washed up on the tide.

'What you doing that for?'

'Because,' replied Laura, seriously, 'it's a game.' Adding, with a wicked grin, 'Didn't anyone ever teach you any games?'

Tom made a face at her. They sat, throwing stones at the bottle for a while, then Tom said, 'What are you going to do now?'

'Sit here for a bit.'

'Ha. Ha.'

'Sorry. That's no way to talk to a boy with a broken head.' She paused. 'We're going back to London, actually.'

'When?'

'Saturday. You see, the light's already fading. It gets even softer come autumn proper. You can't make films without the light.'

'Where will you go?'

'I think we might go to America for the winter. Barney says that actors out there are keen to work in films; not like here, where they think it's the lowest of the low.'

'It won't be the same here, anymore.'

'Barney's keeping the bungalow on. So we'll be back next summer and get another studio built and do even more films. Barney wants to get a cinema in the village.'

'In Aduring?'

'Why not? Anything'd be better than the boathouse.' She looked long and hard at Tom. 'Don't look so down.'

'I shall miss you all.' He paused. 'I shall miss you.'

'It *has* been special, Tom. This summer. It has.' She took his hand.

'You don't seem too sad to be goin'.'

'I'm used to leaving people and places. We do it all the time; we always have – and we go back to places all the time, too. We *will* be back here – come the summer.'

Tom nodded. 'Will you always be an actress?'

I expect so.'

'You never fancied doing anything else?' Tom felt a

sense of familiarity about his question, as if they were words in a play. Then he remembered: he had asked Ern exactly the same questions back at the beginning of the summer.

'Of course I have. I fancied myself as a nun once; then I thought it would be wonderful to work in a shop; then I thought perhaps I'd marry an Earl and run a big country house . . .' Laura laughed. 'I like acting. But then I might give it up I suppose. I don't know. Still there's plenty of time yet.'

And Tom suddenly realised why Laura seemed so different. She wasn't 'the Merrys' girl', like he was still – as Maisie had pointed out – 'the Jupes' boy'. She was not even Miss Adelaide Dupre's Little Jenny Wren anymore.

They had reached a breakwater. Tom was shaken out of his train of thought as Laura cried, 'Hey! Look! Those names are still there, we carved. Lorrilee. Daniel.'

'Do some more?'

'All right.'

They found two sharp flints, and set to work again, this time on the breakwater a little higher up the beach.

'Barney was ever so keen on the *Daniel Lyons* film,' said Laura. 'He'll probably want to finish it when we come back next year – I suppose you'll have to act in it again!'

Tom shook his head. 'I don't want to be an actor.'

Laura's laugh came out a snort. 'You certainly didn't look very comfortable working with Leonora!'

'I wasn't very comfortable,' said Tom with some feeling.

'Oh well, perhaps you'll be able to be a cameraman like Joe.'

'I don't think so,' said Tom quietly. 'I'll be left school, see. I'll be working.'

'Doing what?'

'Well, I got this plan, see.'

'Well, go on, tell us then!'

'You won't split?'

'Who is there to split to?'

'Say Cross me heart and hope to die, burned and tortured if I lie.'

'Oh, all right . . .'

The pact duly made, Tom told Laura his plan in detail.

When they had finished their carving, they walked back to the bungalow.

The two names – 'Laura', 'Tom' – stood out clearly on the breakwater above the incoming tide.

The Jupes sat down to supper one evening in September, just a few weeks after Tom had gone back to school. His father finished grace and suddenly said: 'Your mother and me 'as bin thinkin', boy. About your future.' He hung his fork over the tall glass jar, then pounced and speared a pickled onion. 'I might ha' bin summat hasty about young Puttock's prospects. You know 'e's the official village photographer? 'E seems to be a sensible enough young fellow.'

Tom caught Maisie's eye and she swiftly glanced down at her lump of cheese.

'Though 'e's still too flash by 'alf for my likin',' Mr Jupe added quickly.

'Get on with it, Will,' goaded Mrs Jupe.

'Anyway, the upshot of it is this, boy. If you want an apprenticeship with 'im an' 'e's 'appy to take you on, I'm prepared to discuss terms with 'im.'

Tom looked his father fully in the eye. 'Dad, thanks for the offer like, but I don't think I do. Not anymore.'

Maisie's eyes had popped out on stalks; his mother stopped chewing and looked at Tom, while his father sat motionless as a pickled onion slithered noiselessly and unnoticed off his fork and onto the floor.

'What do you mean, boy? I thought you wanted to be a photographer like Wilf Puttock?'

'Oh, Wilf's all right.' Tom shot a quick glance at Maisie. 'But I got summat else in mind now.'

'Oh . . .?' queried Mr Jupe suspiciously. 'And what might that be?'

'I want an apprenticeship with you in the carpenter's shop.'

Mr Jupe's fork fell out of his hand. 'Well I never did. Well I never did . . .!'

What Tom did not try to explain to his father, though, was that he was 'the Jupes' boy' no longer. Neither did he intend to be 'like' Wilf Puttock, or for that matter 'like' Joe. He had to go his way, do things his way.

Only one person knew just what he thought his way was, and that was Laura. Only she knew that in his mind's eye, Tom saw the rubble of the burnt out South Seas Film studio cleared away and a great new studio erected in its place. And the Guv'nor demanding new wooden sets to be built in the brand new studio. Whole new worlds of pasts, presents and futures.

'I want a one-eyed knife-grinder's parlour in Hackney! And I want it so real it'll shiver every member of the audience out of their seats. Now where's that chief set designer of mine?'

'Yes, Guv'nor?'

'Ah, Tom, dear boy, just the man I've been looking for!'

Barn Owl Books

THE PUBLISHING HOUSE DEVOTED ENTIRELY TO
THE REPRINTING OF CHILDREN'S BOOKS

RECENT TITLES

Arabel's Raven – Joan Aiken

Mortimer the raven is determined to sleep in the bread bin. Mrs Jones says no

Mortimer's Bread Bin – Joan Aiken

Mortimer the raven finds the Joneses and causes chaos in Rumbury Town

The Spiral Stair – Joan Aiken

Giraffe thieves are about! Arabel and her raven have to act fast

Your Guess is as Good as Mine – Bernard Ashley

Nicky gets into a stranger's car by mistake

The Gathering – Isobelle Carmody

Four young people and a ghost battle with a strange evil force

Voyage – Adèle Geras

Story of four young Russians sailing to the U.S. in 1904

Private – Keep Out! – Gwen Grant

Diary of the youngest of six in the 1940s

Leila's Magical Monster Party – Ann Jungman

Leila invites all the baddies to her party and they come!

The Silver Crown – Robert O'Brien

A rare birthday present leads to an extraordinary quest

Playing Beatie Bow – Ruth Park

Exciting Australian time travel story in which Abigail learns about love

The Mustang Machine – Chris Powling

A magic bike sorts out the bullies

The Phantom Carwash – Chris Powling

When Lenny asks for a carwash for Christmas, he doesn't expect to get one, never mind a magic one

The Intergalactic Kitchen – Frank Rodgers

The Bird family plus their kitchen go into outer space

You're Thinking about Doughnuts – Michael Rosen

Frank is left alone in a scary museum at night

Strange Exhange – Pat Thomson

What happens when an alien comes to visit instead of a French boy!

Jimmy Jelly – Jacqueline Wilson

A T.V. personality is confronted by his greatest fan

The Devil's Arithmetic – Jane Yolen

Hannah from New York time travels to Auschwitz in 1942 and acquires wisdom